A Story of Addiction, Forgiveness, and Transformation

ANOTHER ROUND

by Susan P. Waits

PHILOWORKS

Philoworks Publishing LLC

Another Round

Copyright © 2013 by Susan P. Waits

All rights reserved.

ISBN 978-0-9895072-2-6

Library of Congress Control Number: 2013942187

LCCN Imprint Name:
Philoworks Publishing LLC, Memphis, TN

Dedication

For Paul, my twin flame, my husband, without whom this book, and my very life, would never have been complete.

Contents

Preface

This story trickled from me the way water seeps from a very small hole, slow and often imperceptible but forming a puddle nonetheless. It is the same sort of persistent drip than can carve mountains.

Another Round is fiction, but the mental and emotional temper was forged from my personal experience with alcoholism—that of family members and close friends. One of these souls was in his early twenties when the consequences of his addiction led him to the twelve-step program of Alcoholics Anonymous. He once told me, "It's just not fair! Why is it that my friends can drink a few beers and keep it together? But I know I can't. I know I will drink until I pass out. I do it every time."

He was intuitive at an early age. He was very lucky.

Much of this book is inspired by my relationship with my grandmother, though this is not her life story. Most of her adult life was characterized by bouts of uncontrolled binging, and in the face of an atrophic death, she was urged into rehab at the age of sixty-eight. She recovered. As a result, I was gifted the opportunity to know her better than was possible before, and I saw her spirit undiluted, in a fresh light. She was proof that it's never too late to come back into the light, never too late in life for redemption, never too late for "another round."

There were other strands of alcoholism and substance abuse that ran through my family tree, as well as other dramatic examples of reclamation of sobriety and purposefulness. In fact, the original title adopted for the manuscript as it was under development was *Milagros*, which is Spanish for "miracles." It is nothing less than a miracle, an intervention from the spirit that binds us all, to witness a personality transform from unconscious chemical dependence into conscious self-awareness and control.

We all have stories. And we tell them over and over until they become our reality. To let go of a long-held story is akin to letting go of a lover or child. Sometimes it has to be wrenched away. But true freedom is to free the mind and heart from the suppressed traumas still alive in our internal dialogue, and to live authentically and presently, the past gently set aside with utmost respect, a legacy of each individual's wild amalgam of experience.

Another Round is offered to the reader as a gift of hope. To live without guilt and regret is to live with less need for anesthetization, and is the product of love, forgiveness, and release. I know firsthand that it is never too late to let go and let God, to forgive others and ourselves, to open the door to personal transformation. This I truly believe.

Namasté,
Susan

Claire: Land of the Living Dead

How do you pack for prison? My mind was a jumble as I sifted through drawers, throwing the dregs of my wardrobe into an old hard-case Samsonite. My entire wardrobe was decrepit. I hadn't cared about my appearance in a very long time.

So, there I stood, packing for Lord knows how long, soon to be housed like a criminal in a most-certainly-stark, dormitory-type room equipped with a lumpy mattress, sheets as rough as a potato sack, common drunks wandering about, periodic counseling with asinine people, gruel for sustenance: the ultimate betrayal by my family. Why not just handcuff me and put chains around my ankles?

Lord God Almighty, I did not want to go. But I was too old to run, and where would I go? An old woman who wanted to stay comfortably drunk—that was me in a nutshell.

An endless loop of roundabout thoughts ran through my head—a drone of anxiety: *I'm dying, you're dying; we're all dying anyway. Aren't we all headed sooner or later down the very same mortal path? We stop breathing; our hearts stop. Sometimes death comes from a bullet; sometimes it comes from the endless bottoms of glasses of scotch. I choose scotch—or wine or whatever. Dust to damn dust. Why can't they let me be, let me finish out my life in my own time, in my own way? It is my life after all. They have their own lives. I don't need anyone's help with mine.*

The familiar click of the screen door against the frame made my heart leap into my throat. They were here. Jesus. It was time. How had my life devolved to this point? Fear clutched at me, and I desperately wished to fold over and sink down under the water's surface, a slow and peaceful drowning.

"Mother, are you ready?" Daughter Beth's voice was full of nerves and carried an apologetic tone at the same time.

I stood at the top of the stairs, navy pumps, suitcase in tow, head held high, even though exhaustion and waves of nausea rocked me. My abused body systems hungered desperately for numbing relief. It had been eighteen hours since the last scotch—give or take. They had removed every last drop from the house. I felt jittery, panicky, and angry.

I would get through this—or I wouldn't. I would come out on the other side of the nightmare, the land of the living or the dead. That much was certain. But which would it be? I could not imagine life without my daily dose of Usher's Green Stripe, and I really was beyond giving a tinker's damn. Just leave me the hell alone.

༄

Not one word was spoken during the hour-long drive. Not even eye contact. We are very good at silence, my family.

Our son, Andy, drove, elder sister Beth navigating from the passenger side. Andy was suddenly the patriarch. Billy and I had been relegated to the aging-and-infirm-parent category, riding in the back seat, no longer presumed able to make lucid decisions. Andy switched on the hi-fi stereo in his fancy new BMW, searching for distraction from the deafening silence. Rows of soybeans, milo, and rice whipped by, mesmerizing in lush uniformity. I was nearly lulled into disbelief, or at least temporary amnesia, until nausea reared its nasty head again, a sick reminder of where I was headed and why.

As we approached Greenleaf Center, I was struck by the utter plainness of the single-level, mauve brick building that seemed to have shot up like an ugly weed along a flat stretch of highway near Jonesboro, Arkansas. This was it? Lord help me. Beth opened my door, took me by the hand, and led me like a lamb to slaughter. My legs were rubbery, about to give way.

The smell of the place—the feel of it—hit me right away. An antiseptic cloud hovered over body odor and faint whiffs of excrement. Large squares of light-blue-speckled tile lit by an unnatural florescent glow paved a maze of halls that stretched in all directions from a central hub like the legs of a giant cinderblock spider. It was enough to drive a person to drink.

A lanky doctor appeared out of nowhere, a bespectacled, middle-aged man with a shock of wavy, gray hair. His tag read "Garrison B. Kellogg, MD, Director of Psychiatry."

"Greetings, Mrs. Danner," he said with a reassuring mix of calm and aplomb. "Welcome to Greenleaf." His arms spread expansively like the lord of a great manor. "And welcome, family." Dr. Kellogg reached an outstretched hand toward Billy, then Andy. Beth forced a smile and nodded in acknowledgment.

"So, here is how it works initially," the doctor began. His lack of a southern accent, or really any accent, obscured his place of origin. "On the first day, good-byes should be very brief. We find this is better for everyone. No visits during the first week. After that, visits will be limited to one hour each day, and of course, in time you will see each other in family counseling."

Quiet engulfed our little circle, cutting through the background noise of chatting staff and ringing phones.

"We understand," Andy said at last. Billy stared at the floor. I'm sure he couldn't bring himself to look into my eyes.

"Could we help her get settled in her room?" Beth asked. "I don't think she feels well."

"We'll take care of everything," Dr. Kellogg assured. "No need to worry."

Andy stepped toward me, circled an arm around my shoulders, and dutifully kissed my cheek. "Mother, we love you and we'll see you very soon." He immediately started toward the door.

"Love you, Mother," Beth said softly and pulled me close. "It's for the best. We all believe that." Tears streamed down her cheeks as she joined her brother. I was angry with them. How could they?

Maybe Billy would rescue me, I thought. He'd always saved me ...

But my husband of forty-two years took my hands and pulled them together at his lips. "Claire, honey, it will be all right. I love you."

I pulled him a few steps away from the group. "Please, Billy, take me home. You don't have to do this."

"I can't, dear. You know that. This will all be behind us before we know it."

With that he turned and walked away.

"This will be behind *us*?" I was the one being left alone in this hellhole. No *us* about it.

ᖆᖇ

"Well now, Claire," Dr. Kellogg began, "we are truly happy to have you here. Please allow me to personally show you to your room. A nurse will follow shortly, and she'll orient you—take you on a tour of the entire facility if you're up to it."

I didn't say a word in response, nor did I look into his eyes as he turned to study me. He walked with his hands clasped low behind his back, pushing the angle of his form forward, ensuring that his head would be the first body part to cross a threshold. A very stereotypical, psychobabbling doctor, I thought.

Patients wandered the halls, willy-nilly, it seemed. And they were nothing like me. Most of them were much younger. As one would expect, they each seemed disturbed and some, downright crazy. One man in particular completely unnerved me with his wild, Einstein hair, Cheshire-cat smile, and pursuant gaze. Mental note number one: stay away from Crazy Hair.

"Ah. Here we are, room 107. And your roommate is a very nice lady named Connie Babcock. I believe she's outside in the common area taking in some fresh air at the moment."

Dr. Kellogg stood patiently, shifting his weight to and fro in shoes that were a bit too shiny. I could feel his eyes trying to commune with mine. He seemed to be expecting a word, but I simply couldn't deal with conversation. I sat down on my assigned bed, folded my hands in my lap, and waited for his next move. Sweat trickled down my spine. After a while, he spoke.

"Very well. I'll send Nurse O'Brien your way. She'll answer any questions you might have, talk with you about our routine, our facility, medication, and the like. Please understand that we are here to help, Claire. You must know that. We'll schedule your first session with me when you begin to feel better physically. I'll be checking on you every day and look forward to the genesis of your recovery."

He touched my shoulder with one finger, wheeled around, and left the room head first. I distinctly remember the "perclap" of his shoes fading into the long tiled hallway.

I was not prone to fits of anger, but at that moment rage and betrayal as I had never known rushed through me like hot lava. If I could have found anything worth smashing, I would have hurled it against the wall right then. If I could have thrown my old body through the barred window and escaped, I would have. If a family member had been near—any one of them—I would have pummeled him or her in the chest with every ounce of remaining energy in my shaky flesh.

That level of rage wanes fairly quickly, though, and gives way to exhaustion. Such intense emotions need an outlet lest they fester. But in my book, ladies do not lose their temper, at least not in front of anyone. My lifelong habit had been to push dark thoughts back down and shroud them with a balm of brain-deadening libation.

At that moment I was beyond desperate for a drink, and if I'd had the physical constitution, I would have escaped the asylum like that big Indian in *One Flew Over the Cuckoo's Nest*. As I waited interminably for Nurse Ratchet, my racing heart slowed, and my fists began to unclench.

From what I could observe, my roommate was somewhat younger and likely had a sordid personal history that I would surely be subjected to in the dark of night. Her side of the room had little in the way of personal effects: a lone, creased photograph of two teenage girls and a few paperbacks on the nightstand. A threadbare robe hung on the outside of the bathroom door. I imagined we'd have little in common, except for the grim fact of being marooned on this unholy island.

Then, like an apparition, a woman dressed in white appeared in the doorway smiling in an almost mischievous way.

"Well, well, well. Ms. Claire Danner. Aren't you the sweetest little woman who's come our way in *such* a long time! I know a true southern belle when I see one. My, my." She shook her head back and forth as she spoke. "I'm Sissy O'Brien, and I'll be taking care of you during your stay."

Short, bleached-blond curls sprang in all directions, and a smile spread magnanimously into the space around her face, spilling onto me like gold dust. A tray teetered on the palm of one hand, and a packet of paperwork was tucked under the same arm, leaving a free hand. If she had laughed out loud for no reason, I would not have been surprised.

I smiled back—a reflex really, like a blink. Her presence was so intensely positive that my comfort level lifted a few notches. "I am incredibly thirsty," I told her. "Just parched."

"I understand," she began. "There is bottled water and juice in your fridge, but take small sips; don't overdo it, and hopefully it will stay down. If you can't keep anything down, we'll start an IV to get you hydrated, as well as tranquilizers if necessary."

Nurse O'Brien sat her tray on top of the compact refrigerator and reached in for water, unscrewing the top for me. "Remember, just a tiny sip at a time until we see."

I took a sip, and my stomach clenched and protested.

"Now I know how hard this is, Claire, because I've been where you are. I want you to hear me when I say those words. *I have been where you are.* I understand like you can't believe."

This surprised me. She looked too young, too vibrant, too damn … cheerful.

"You're in a benevolent place," she continued, "a place where you can come out on the other side if you choose. And that's the key. How this plays out is up to you—completely up to you."

She peered into my eyes then, making her point. "For the first week or so, you can expect to feel much worse before you feel better. Symptoms vary widely. You might feel shaky and dizzy, have bowel disruptions, nausea, chills, sweating, anxiety. You may even have hallucinations. I'll be at your side to give you whatever will help. I'll hold your hand, wipe your face, and dry your tears. And believe you me, there will be tears, buckets and buckets of them, or at least we should hope so. We all have things that are begging for forgiveness. But you *will* get through this."

I stared down at the floor, unable to meet her gaze.

"Claire, you have a chance to be healthy again. You have a lot of good years ahead of you." She bent down at eye level and held both my hands, prodding me to look into her face. Tears of exhaustion welled in my eyes as I revisited her countenance, a spirit that wanted to touch mine, in her hazel eyes an unconditional intention to help and heal and a depth of commitment that did indeed evoke a soul recovered from the abyss. I felt my shoulders drop in resignation and surrendered to the care of this good woman.

"I think I'm going to need that tranquilizer."

"Of course. It'll help with the nausea and help you to relax. And I'll be here to check on you every hour tonight."

A skeletal figure walked through the door, and Sissy greeted her by name. Her ash-blond hair was brittle and thin, and the lines on her face were more pronounced than mine, though she must have been two decades younger. She looked fragile enough to break in two—so fragile that it made me nervous to look at her.

"Connie, this is your new roommate, Claire."

"Pleased to meet you," Connie said with a nod and no change of pace as she headed into the bathroom and closed the door.

"Connie has been here three weeks," Sissy explained. "She's a methamphetamine addict. She is actually doing really well."

After a flush, Connie reappeared and sat Indian-style on her bed.

"OK, Claire, I'm going to let you get settled in and rest. I'll be right back with something to help you feel better. This button right here is your lifeline to me. Call as often as you need. Tomorrow, we'll get to a full work-up of tests, but it's too late for that today. Any questions, dear?"

"Could you go ahead and kill me and get it over with? Any drug will do."

"Not a chance," Sissy replied with a wry smile.

She patted my back and departed, and I was left sitting face to face with a stranger named Connie.

"Please excuse me." I pulled the privacy curtain between our beds, slipped off my shoes, and crawled between the sheets fully clothed. One tranquilizer later—Sissy was quick—exhaustingly fitful sleep overtook me. I hovered in that wretched state between sleeping and waking, tossed about by rough mental seas, my thoughts and dreams senseless and incoherent.

Long, long miserable hours later, the determined sun rose. I was awakened by a bladder full enough to burst and a dull ache in my left arm. My mouth was dry as cotton. I squinted to make out the IV needle plunged deep into a vein in the crook of my left arm. A patch of old skin crinkled like a frown under white tape, and tubes snaked from under the sleeve of a gown. How and when all of that happened was a mystery.

I sat up in bed, and the pain of an imminent explosion within my abdomen trumped any ability to consider the logistics of a trip to the bathroom. I don't really know what happened—a tangle of nightgown, curtain, and tubes. The whole mess hit the tile floor in a crashing heap, and the cold steel of the rolling IV pole beaned me on the head. The blow began to throb through my temples, and pain shot through a bloody left forearm, the needle and tube ripped loose. Lying there helpless in such a state, I began to pee on myself; I could not control it or the sobs that shuddered from my desire at that moment to give up on this pitiful life.

Sissy moved through the door like a wave of light. I remember her smiling gently and knowingly as she began to unravel the mess of me. "We're going to have to teach you how to drive that thing."

"I am so embarrassed. I want to die."

"Tough, tough day for you, I know."

I was thankful that Connie was not present to witness the humiliating experience of Sissy changing my gown and cleaning my privates. It was humiliating enough to become such a burden for Sissy, or anyone for that matter. I vowed that if I was not going to be well, then there was no way in hell I was going to linger in my old age to the point of needing bedpans and diapers. No way.

After Sissy got me settled back in bed with fresh IV and antiseptic for the abrasion on my forehead, she asked, "How are you feeling?"

"Not worth a damn," I mumbled. The knot on my head began to awaken.

"Claire, you had a little spill. You're going to be just fine. I need to check your vitals; then we'll try another trip to the bathroom. This time I'll drive."

Sissy slipped a blood-pressure cuff onto my right arm, and the familiar pumping and squeezing began.

"I can go to the bathroom by myself, you know."

"I realize that, but until you get used to navigating with this pole—and you feel a bit stronger—I'll need to help you get situated. You can shut the door and have your privacy. It won't be that bad. I promise."

I began to cry then, deep and low, a sad, sad song. Sissy pulled me close.

Grace: Altered States

It was so unexpected. That's all I can say.

My summer had been spent like a nomad, thin legs peddling on the orange ten-speed handed down from my sister. Days were long and sun drenched and safe as I disappeared daily on my bike. My mother really had no idea where I ventured, and I don't remember what filled her summer minutes and hours in those days. Sometimes my bike path led to a friend's house to play Barbies or watch soap operas, and other days I joined the throngs of children in the blue-green, over-chlorinated water of Tillman Park pool, surrounded by cracked concrete with little weeds poking through.

But on that day, I decided to visit Mama Claire—unannounced. I had never done so before, and I didn't mention it to Mom. There was really no forethought. I guess it was meant to happen.

Mama Claire's house had always been such a loving haven of high ceilings, wood floors, and mint-green walls, the smell of my grandfather's pipe tobacco permeating everything.

As I walked in, I was greeted with a whoosh of silence, like I had entered a vacuum. Or maybe my mind wrapped up the memory like that.

"Mama Claire?" The rubber soles of my tennis shoes squeaked on the polished hardwood. "Mama? Are you home?"

She appeared, but this was not my Mama Claire—not as I had ever known her in my ten years on this planet. She was slightly disheveled and so fluid in movement and speech that I thought she might melt into a puddle in front of me as she swept me into an uncomfortable embrace.

"Honey! I didn't hear you come in," she drawled. As she led me to the chair in front of the antique vanity in her guest bedroom, I noticed bare feet and chipped, burgundy nail polish on crooked, neglected toes. She had never been barefoot—not that I remembered. I had never seen her feet, anyway. She took a silver-plated brush from the drawer and began to very slowly, very deliberately brush and stroke my hair. She was another character completely, hijacked by an alternate personality, who had transformed my grandmother into someone unrecognizable—not someone terrible, just radically different.

"You're the most beautiful one in the family, you know that, don't you?"

As she ran the brush through my hair, I considered her words and pondered my reflection, and hers, in the mirror. Her lipstick was classic red against alabaster skin, jagged outside the line of her upper lip. The pupils in her dark eyes were huge. A curl of graying hair dangled low on her forehead as she leaned in. Her breath was pungent, unpleasant. "You are the one. Yes, you are. The most special of all."

Her words hung in the air like overripe fruit. Were they true? Was I really that special? I loved her. I looked up to her in ways that I wasn't even aware of at the time. Was she believable in this altered state? What in the world had taken hold of her? The questions spun in my head and compelled me to sprint out the door and not look back.

"I have to go, Mama Claire." I edged out of the chair uneasily.

"No, honey. Stay. I want you to stay." She laid a firm hand on my shoulder.

"Nope. I can't. Sorry." Her arms circled around me again, and I slipped through the unsteady embrace, the back door in sight. "I'll see you later, though. I promise. Mom needs me home now."

I closed the door behind me and gulped the humid air, my heart racing. I rode home fast, the wind in my face erasing the unfamiliar smells, clearing my head.

My instinct was not to cry. There were no tears. But the experience jarred me down deep, an unwelcome realization that everything is not always what you expect or have come to believe. It was a lesson that even the people held most dear can change, or things can change people; that everything is not steadfast, even grandmothers.

ᏇᎧ

"Miss. *Miss.*" A hand touched my shoulder, and my eyes blinked open as I came back to the present. "Please raise your seat to the upright position. We'll be landing soon."

I hadn't thought about that seminal event with Mama Claire in years. Actually, I had never thought of it as seminal before.

I closed the book in my lap and noticed that the strange little bald man next to the window had turned my way and was leering at me, a speck of peppercorn stuck between two front teeth. God, I could not wait to be off the plane.

I was twenty-one, returning home after six blissful weeks in San Miguel de Allende, Mexico, on an exchange program for art students. My plan was to spend several weeks at home with my family in northeast Arkansas before returning to Rhodes College in Memphis for my senior year.

Suffice it to say, my mood and my Spanish were much improved after that journey to Mexico's left ventricle. After all, San Miguel was home to my first lover, Javier, a stunning man with classically handsome features, eyes that left me undone, and a body that still rocked me with requited desire. I might never see him again. I didn't know.

Seven years older and experienced in the art of pleasuring a woman, Javier taught me to let go. I opened up like a flower, and my nectar he drank. I was changed; I felt grown up, worldly, even a bit enlightened. Although looking back, my libido was the primary inheritor of the light.

Long, lazy mornings in San Miguel were spent sipping coffee in cafés along the manicured plaza under cerulean skies, and having esoteric conversations with local intelligentsia about art and, most importantly, who was sleeping with whom. Balmy afternoons found me with a sketchpad or canvas trying to capture the intricacies of a Gothic cathedral spire or an ancient cobblestone street as narrow as a needle's eye with a view of a rolling landscape stretching languidly beyond.

But my days were also spent rehydrating, allowing my small body to recover from the nightly punishment of partying. Almost every night, partying.

My family was a hard-drinking lot, including me. I actually can't remember a time when the people around me were not drinking for some reason. Every celebration or gathering warranted a cocktail in one's hand, and it was actually a family faux pas not to acquiesce. So it was natural that I would be curious about my family's drug of choice at an early age.

My first time to overindulge was at age fourteen on a family trip to Washington, DC. At dinner one night in the Old Ebbitt Grill, as the adults were completely wrapped up in conversation and inebriation, the wine glass in front of me was filled and refilled. I did not object. No one noticed that I could barely walk out of the restaurant. And so the pattern emerged like an insidious thought that corrupts if given enough attention.

I returned from San Miguel with the realization that maybe it was time to modify my drinking habits. Travel can inspire that kind of insight—a seed with the potential to take root. When I later found out about Mama Claire's intervention, the impulse to reassess was affirmed, at least temporarily. But much like a New Year's resolution that gets forgotten before the end of January, a real reassessment needs the fuel of some imminent and adverse consequence to give it substance. What is an addiction anyway but something that begins as pleasure but over time is abused to the point of creating pain, to the point of losing one's control over the experience? Right then my liver was plenty strong, and I was having way too much fun. No pain.

Of course, I couldn't wait to visit Mama Claire, hoping beyond hope that she wasn't drinking. She could be so much fun and would appreciate a recounting of my Mexican adventure more than anyone else. I envisioned us sipping iced tea laced with sprigs of the fresh mint that grew wild behind her house. We'd sit on the back-porch swing and spin tales embellished for the pure entertainment of each other.

I had made peace in my later teenage years with her addiction, though I still felt the pull to quiz her about her past—about what made her want to periodically disappear from her life. Finding just the right time to ask was important because she could be so private and feline. She had to be in the mood.

After a restful night's sleep, which rejuvenated me after my long trip, I sat in sock feet at the breakfast table of my childhood, nibbling on the crust of a piece of wheat toast. Mom lingered in her ratty, pink chenille robe, happy to have me home.

I hadn't asked about Mama Claire in months—way before I'd left for Mexico. The rigorous demands of school, my job as a hostess at Friday's on Overton Square, and my budding social life were all consuming. Plus, I figured things were about the same anyway. Ask and ye shall know.

"So, how's Mama Claire and Pop? Same old, same old? Thought I'd visit her today. Take some trip photos by."

The light fell from Mom's face. A decade of new worry lines seemed to materialize.

"She's worse, Grace, really, I'm sorry to say. I noticed a real downturn after Byhalia passed away. She's drinking all the time now—hardly gets out of bed. I didn't want to worry you; that's why I haven't said anything. We're at the point where something has got to be done. Dr. Jackson came to the house to see her this week. Said she's suffering from malnutrition and slowly killing herself. He strongly recommended we get professional help with her addiction."

I was not surprised by the news. Dismayed, of course, but not surprised. I had watched Mama Claire's self-punishment my whole life. Actually I was relieved that some course of action was in the works.

"What are you going to do? What can you do?"

"An inpatient setting of some sort. That's what Andy and I believe anyway. She'll never agree to it—that's putting it mildly. We know her well enough to know she'll be mad as hell—dig her stubborn heels in the dirt. We'd be committing her. But her health is at stake, Grace. Convincing Pop to go along was the first step, and he's barely on board. Andy and I are going to their house tomorrow night for an intervention with Mother. We're planning to take her to the Greenleaf clinic in Jonesboro."

Mom bowed her head and kneaded the skin on her forehead.

"So you talked to Pop? How'd he take it?

"Well, we waited until the end of a workday and went by his office. Actually, he didn't seem surprised at all—like he knew it was coming. It was so sad really; he seemed old and pitiful in his oversized lab coat, sort of hunched over and resigned to it all."

"What did he say?"

"Not much. He just listened. Said it was a decision he couldn't have made on his own."

She sighed and rummaged through the kitchen junk drawer until her hidden stash of Virginia Slims emerged. I hadn't seen her smoke in forever. She lit one and took a long drag.

"Oh, Mom. I'm so sorry. How can I help? You know I'll do anything I can."

"Thank you, sweetie, but this is my problem. I've been in denial, but it's time."

"I'm still going to go see her today. I need to see her."

"Don't do it, Grace. It's not pretty. And she probably won't even remember you came by. Save yourself the anguish."

"I'll think about it," I told her but knew all along I'd go, mule-stubborn soul that I am. It runs in the family.

◌◌

Mom was right. It wasn't pretty. Not in any light. It was downright scary. Mama Claire was wearing light-blue, double-knit pants with an overstretched elastic waist, her belly bulging from an otherwise tiny form. (I later learned this was a sign of severe malnutrition.) A frayed satin pajama top bared an aging breast as she shifted position. She sat with one leg dangling over the arm of a worn chintz wingback chair in her bedroom—a pose that absolutely would never have happened in her right mind. Still salt and pepper, her hair was oily and unruly. All of her, in fact, seemed oily and unruly.

Our exact conversation is a bit of a blur; it was quietly incoherent and disturbing. The next night, Mama Claire's family-practice doctor joined Mom, Uncle Andy, and Pop for the intervention.

Mom later told me Mama Claire was in a stupor and expressed almost no emotion—sat catatonic. She agreed with everything that night just to get them off her back, but the next morning was a different story. She was indignant, stated flatly she was not going.

It was Uncle Andy who changed her tune. He pleaded with her, reminded her that she had made a promise the night before. Apparently he reminded his mother of a lifetime of broken promises, all forgotten in the fog of intoxication. It must have softened her resolve.

As Mom was describing these events, I thought of a pack of animals, how the strong ones coerce the weak into submission. The addict is surrounded, nowhere to turn. The will of the pack is inescapable.

Mama Claire was escorted to rehab that day—at age sixty-eight.

Claire: A Life Long Lost

The bed was a foreign country, as was the very air in that sordid place. The woman named Connie snored lightly in her slumber, mumbled incoherently now and then. Her presence was wildly irritating. Where were the private rooms?

My anxiety level had ratcheted up steadily all day, along with bouts of sweating and nausea. I still hadn't left the room. Connie had stayed away as much as she could, thank God. At least I was managing to get to the bathroom without assistance or another incident.

At lights-out, Sissy blessedly dosed me with something. I felt loopy but better.

Random memories, dark vignettes of my life, surrounded me like a veil. Most were downright horrible experiences that had been tucked away for decades and held hostage by the alcohol gods, a selfish lot who entice with the hot liquid lure of escape. They kill. They kill vital cells. They kill awareness. Yet, they also kept me screaming for more, more! Anesthetize me. Bathe me with amnesia. Kill the demons deep within me, please.

I thought of Byhalia—she'd practically raised Beth and Andy. I remembered the day she came into our lives and rescued my new baby Beth from my ineptitude, my addictions. I am forever indebted to her. Oh, how I miss her …

Then I became lost in thoughts of Henry, with whom my life began … and ended. The night we met came rushing back, visceral:

There I was, the picture of youth and vitality. It was 1934, and I was studying at Brenau in Atlanta. His fraternity at Emory hosted a dance in the ballroom of the Ansley Hotel. Our eyes connected from across the crowded room during a lull in the music. He walked straight toward me, Henry Paul Robison III, took my hand, and introduced himself. It was as if the whole world stopped in that instant—noise, movement, thought. All the girls flitting around in gowns became frozen in time, like so many beautiful ornaments. I could not speak. My heart pounded wildly in my throat. *Sweet Jesus.* There was something about his eyes. Oh my God, his eyes. They were blue, blue and peered into the deepest part of me. I have not looked at anything or anyone quite the same since.

I did not know I was a virgin until that moment—physically, spiritually, emotionally. I instinctively knew that if he asked me to board a long boat to China, I would go. If he reached under my gown and touched my intimate places, I would shiver and completely give in to the desires we both felt. I just knew.

We made love that night in a room at the Ansley. We barely knew each other's personality, but we knew each other intimately by soul. The experience was the most intense and exquisite of my life, and at the same time as natural as breathing. A primordial rhythm flowed through us, a timeless dance that must have begun in another eon, another universe.

From that night on, we were inseparable—together whenever we could be, never for a moment imagining anything other than a continuation of the beauty of our first night. And for nine glorious months, we lived and breathed each other, barely studying, skipping classes, and retaining just enough to get by. We spent time with his family on weekends, a tribe of native Georgians with roots as deep as an old oak and the warmest hospitality I'd ever encountered. Sometimes we'd jaunt off on spur-of-the-moment train journeys to wonderful places like Charleston, spending most of our time in the bedroom, loving and laughing and merging as one, slipping out of our cocoon only occasionally to stroll nearby and forage for sustenance.

The miracle of Henry and me was this: he could see through the looking glass, through my convoluted and insecure veneer to the authentic me, the timeless soul of me. He understood. He simply, effortlessly, could *see* me and I him in exactly the same way, like two mirrors facing each other reflecting infinite love in both directions. It was a pure connection of spirits. Until then I had only heard of love at first sight and thought such was a myth, something made up by the poets and the romance novelists. But in Henry I immediately and instinctively knew I had met the twin of my soul. It wasn't so much a falling in love with someone new as it was discovering and recognizing a long-lost love.

And then he died. My Henry died one late fall day in the deer woods. I remember the way he looked when he left that morning: flannel shirt, dark hair curling at his neck, morning beard. He leaned down to kiss me good-bye and smoothed my hair with his hand. He kissed me again; then I heard him unbuckle the belt holding his khaki hunting pants on his slim hips, and he climbed on top of me, unable to resist one more lovemaking session before leaving. It was the last time I saw him alive.

Somehow, unfathomably, in a hardwood forest some fifty miles from the nearest hospital, his friend Tony's gun discharged accidentally. Henry bled to death before they could get him to a hospital. There is no doubt that Tony and Morgan valiantly tried to save him, putting pressure on the gaping hole, pleading with every ounce of energy for him to hold on.

๑๑

In my drug-induced state, it was difficult to discern memory from nightmare as my subconscious created an alternate reality. In my delirium Henry's death played out quite differently:

Henry and I were sitting on a dock with our toes stirring the water. The air was heavy with a fog so dense we could only see the space between our faces in the wet cloud surrounding us. We touched fingers and sat wordlessly. There was no need for words.

Henry whispered in my ear, "It's time, Claire. I don't know why; I can't explain it yet, but it's time. But *know* that we will be together again. *Know it.*" He took both of my hands and squeezed. "*We are one.* Please allow joy in this life." With that he stood and fell face first into the calm water, sinking, sinking.

I screamed, "No, *no!*" and jumped in after him, swimming and diving, searching for him. But he was gone. Suddenly I felt the pressure of the water as I sank deeper, the light from the surface fading. I felt it—the sweet pull of death. It wasn't as scary as I imagined. It was as though I were choosing between two worlds.

Then panic set in, and my will to live thrust my body upward, lungs on fire, back to this world. I awoke with a start, heart racing, gasping for air, sheets wet with sweat. I hadn't dreamed about him in years and years.

"Are you OK? Should I call Sissy?" Connie's voice came from behind the curtain.

"No. No. I'm OK," I lied. "Just a bad dream." The truth was, I was not OK and felt I had just seen my own death. And dying right then did not seem like such a bad idea.

The feel of Henry's presence was still with me, lingering like the scent of sex, the special air of his touch palpable. God, how I missed him, even after all these years, which now found me an elderly woman drowning here in a pool of mildewed dreams.

Grace: Surrogate Mothers

That night, I could not shake the disheveled image of Mama Claire and the way she seemed so disconnected, so unlike the grandmother I had created in my memory. And in the morning haze before fully waking, my recollection of that summer day in 1976 came alive again, the day I first learned of Mama Claire's drinking problem. In my mind's eye, it was like watching Dad's old reel-to-reel:

"So how are you, Miss Grace Anne?" Mom asked, innocent to my trauma.

Emotion shot through me as I moved through the room in a blur. Something about Mom asking me if I was OK had always seemed to undo me. She was pressed against the sink peeling potatoes, scarf around her hair, plaid blouse tied across curvy hips.

"Just peachy, Mom. Gotta get something in my room. Be out in a minute."

Whew. Escape. No real interactions with anyone. I sat on my bed with my legs pulled in tight and studied the abstract flowers in the wallpaper. My mind was a mess, eyes tracing indefinite patterns of petals and stems.

I couldn't shake the feeling that I had done something wrong. I felt sort of dirty. Had anyone else seen her like that? Was it something about me that made her act like a stranger?

Mama Claire had taken care of me—good care of me—from the time I was really little. She'd taught me proper manners. "Yes, ma'am, no, ma'am, thank you, ma'am, please," she would say, and then praise me when I repeated her words. She played tea party, not tiring at all as I elaborately set up dolls and stuffed animals around a tiny table. She giggled and sighed elaborately as we tried valiantly to teach etiquette to our furry guests. She was always ready for a game of cards and would curl up at bedtime to read long stories from books she'd saved from Mom's childhood. She drew baths for me in the old claw-footed tub and let me soak as long as I wanted in lavender-scented water. Her small hands rubbed my legs at night when awful growing pains made me moan. When she leaned in to kiss my forehead, her perfume was lovely.

A bath—yes, a bath was just the ticket. *Just wash it all away.* Cross the hall; look both ways. Thankfully, no one was within sight. *Lock the bathroom door. Deep breath.* As I leaned over to turn the spigot, Elizabeth barged in. The lock in that old bathroom door had never worked right, and Dad never got around to fixing it.

"A little privacy here!"

"Oh, Grace, please. You're just a skinny string bean with absolutely no boobs."

"Please," I begged. "Get out, Elizabeth. *Get out!*"

"You OK?" she asked. My eyes brimmed with tears. "What's wrong, Sis?"

I pulled off my khaki shorts, T-shirt, my cotton panties dotted with little pastel ice cream cones, and dipped a finger into the liquid warmth. "I don't know if I can tell you. It's too weird. You'll think so."

"OK, then. Get in and pull the curtain and pretend I'm not here and just say it. I promise I won't think it's weird."

"You will. I know you will." I paused. Sighed. Gathered up my courage like a worn security blanket and climbed into the bath. Knobby white knees floated above shins covered in greenish-blue kid bruises. My sister was uncharacteristically silent. "Elizabeth, I rode my bike to Mama Claire's today, and something was bad wrong with her. Really wrong. It freaked me out."

"Did you tell Mom?"

"No … I was afraid to."

"Well, Grace …" She paused for what seemed like forever. "OK. I don't know if I should be the one to tell you this—I didn't know it for a long time, either—but Mama Claire drinks too much sometimes. When she's drinking, Mom has always just kept us away."

"What do you mean, she drinks? You mean alcohol? You're saying she was drunk today? Mama Claire? No way!"

But something in me said it made sense.

"Yes, way. You know I wouldn't kid you about something like that. She sometimes drinks for weeks, then stops and gets on with her life like nothing has happened. I've seen it, Sis. No one knows why—well, maybe someone knows, but I don't. But it makes Mom sad. She's used to it, though. Mama Claire did it when Mom was little, too."

"Really? Geez. *Geez.*" All I could do was shake my head back and forth behind the shower curtain. "How'd you find out?"

"A few years ago we stopped by—Mom didn't know she was drinking. You were too little to notice, but Mom had to explain it to me. She had tears in her eyes when she told me, said I shouldn't think less of Mama Claire, that she's a fine lady with an illness. She said it's like being sick. Mom said everyone has faults, and Mama Claire is just not strong when it comes to drinking. When she starts she has trouble stopping. It's OK, Grace, really. Don't worry about it too much."

But I did worry. I needed to talk with Byhalia about it. She'd know what to do. Byhalia had worked for Mama Claire for about a hundred years.

∞

"Byhalia, I really love you," I told her as she flipped corn-cakes over a simple gas flame at her house in colored town. Sometimes she let me spend a weekend night, and we did a whole lot of nothing. Those are some of my favorite memories.

Her yard was mostly dirt underneath a giant magnolia that was as old as God himself. Her hound dog, Rex, spent most of his entire life in that spot, sometimes chained up, eating greasy leftovers, scratching fleas, and getting his ears rubbed. We spent our time sipping sweet tea and lounging in aluminum lawn chairs straight from the Sears & Roebuck catalog store. Byhalia looked like she was going to pop right through the woven green-and-white-striped nylon seat.

We gossiped about everyone who walked by. Byhalia knew all the inside stories, the nooks and crannies of lives. Her cracked Formica kitchen table was practically a coun-seling center for her neighbors, who felt a special freedom to share intimate details and soak up homespun wisdom. There was always someone popping by.

"Oh, sweet girl, I love you, too. You're so much like your mama when she was your age—Lord knows I can't tell you," she said, laughing with her mouth wide open.

She was pretty old by then with a stiff, arthritic limp. I'd always thought her limp might have something to do with the ultra tight knee-high nylons she wore every day under her dresses. They looked painful, like any minute they'd cut her large legs straight off just below the knee. I imagined that when she rolled those things down at night, the deep grooves in her flesh stayed until morning, never quite recovering from the tourniquet grip.

Her dentures shifted endearingly as she spoke—that is, when she chose to wear them. Mostly she went around toothless and was refreshingly unselfconscious about the nakedness of her mouth. As she spoke, I studied the prominent ridges in her bluish-brown gums where teeth had once been lodged. I was thinking about how I might want to be a dentist when I grew up. I'd fix Byhalia's teeth for free, and those of other old people with naked mouths. How in the world could they chew pork chops?

She still worked a couple of days a week for my grandparents, but she didn't really do much anymore—a little laundry and ironing, a dust mop flopped here and there, a washed dish or two. Mostly, she and Mama Claire enjoyed each other's company, but if you asked them they'd probably pretend it wasn't so.

I felt so close to her, like there was nothing I couldn't ask, and I needed her perspective. She knew Mama Claire better than anyone.

"Byhalia, I've been wanting to ask you something. It's about Mama Claire."

The skin framing her watery brown eyes was sketched with a map of weariness that I noticed for the first time. It made me feel that I should never burden her.

"I been knowing this day would come," she said, a huge sigh moving her giant bosoms up and down in an exaggerated way. "You want to know about Mama Claire's drinking, don't you?" I nodded. "Right after you went and seen her the other day—and, sweet girl, I wish I had been there and none of that would have happened—and you told Elizabeth and Elizabeth told your Mama and your Mama told it to me, I been waiting to talk with you about it."

"Why does she do it if it changes her? That's what I want to know. And why does she do it when it makes everyone so sad?"

"There ain't no easy answer for that. It's like asking why the sun shines or why the moon gets full. It's a mystery why some people take a drink and they can't stop. They just drink and drink until they pass flat out. They don't want to keep on, but they driven to. I don't rightly know why. Maybe they got bad feelings they need to keep on covering up, again and again.

"But what if they don't drink at all? How about that? Why can't Mama Claire just drink tea and Cokes and be happy—like the rest of us?"

"Because, sweet child, she been drinking for years, and if she stops, she gets real sick. It ain't pretty. She'd have to go to the hospital to stop for good."

"Well then, let's take her, today. Right this minute," I said with conviction, rising from the kitchen table.

"We can't, sugar. *She* has to decide to stop. Herself. Can't nobody do that for her."

"How do you know?"

"I just do, child. I've lived a long time, seen lots of people be sick with it. Every now and again, people decide to quit, and they change their lives for the better. But most don't. It's how they live for good."

"But why do people change so much? Why do they act like different people when they drink?"

"Cause it messes with your mind, alcohol does. Listen, we all love your Mama Claire just the way she is. And she loves you and Elizabeth more than the world. She's doing real good right now. Ask your mama to take you 'round to see her later. It would mean a lot, sugar."

Claire: Marooned in the Abyss

Hot water pulsed on my back in the claustrophobic shower of my meager accommodations. My thirsty pores opened in the moist heat, as did my mind. And the past kept rushing back, insistent as hell, forcing me to deal with … me, unlibated and undiluted. And if I let my past truly sink into my awareness—felt the groaning agony of it—I loathed myself. I had selfishly allowed other people to pick up the pieces of whatever I'd managed to break, or leave undone: Byhalia, Billy, my children, my grandchildren.

Could they ever forgive me? Could I forgive myself?

Another wave of profound exhaustion and despair descended on me, close kin to the raw emotion bubbling up from where it had been stuffed down and plastered over for decades. Hell hath no fury like an old body weaning itself from an almost-constant drip of alcohol. I craved my anesthetic and would have handed my soul to the devil for a generous scotch in a cut-glass highball, neat.

It was barely dawn—four days since being marooned here—the first day of one-on-one counseling with Dr. Kellogg. I dreaded what he would try to dredge up from my emotional grave full of brittle bones and decayed secrets.

Before the expected exhumation of my past, I hungered for fresh air and sky—a reprieve from the sterile, regimented world of a rehab clinic and the oppressive confines of a dingy dorm room with twin hospital beds. I decided to make my way to the sad little courtyard with its view of a scum-covered pond. It would have to do. At least I could see the sky.

Staff milled about silently as I meandered through the maze of identical hallways. No patients roamed the halls yet, thank God. I had kept to myself almost completely so far, taking what little broth and food I'd been able to keep down in the privacy of my room. Connie was good about letting me be, even as I snapped at her and vomited in the bedpan. She understood.

As I opened the door to the courtyard, the cool morning air kissed my skin. I shut my eyes and breathed deeply, a wee bit thankful that the throbbing in my head and the wrenching in my gut had somewhat subsided. A concrete bench in one corner called to me as a blue jay landed on the birdfeeder at the center of the yard. The bird eyed me curiously as he nibbled on breakfast, his head cocked this way and that in contemplative curiosity. I moved carefully to the bench so as not to disturb him, and he flew over and landed right beside me, a miracle of sorts. I held my breath and closed my eyes, willing him to stay.

It looks like I'm going to live after all, in spite of myself. God, if you are there, please help me. And forgive me for everything. I'm tired of remembering, tired of the demons, tired of the shame. I just want peace. I really have no good reason to carry on.

I opened my eyes. No blue jay. Something in the far corner caught my attention—wild gray hair. Damn it. Einstein hair. He saw me and began to amble in my direction. Damn it. I'd avoided him so far.

"Well, hello, pretty lady. What brings you out so early?"

"Not conversation."

"Ah-ha. A feisty one. I like that."

"You like nothing of the kind, mister."

One side of his face twitched as he studied me. His lips were deeply cracked and coated in thick saliva. But his eyes unnerved me most of all.

"Maybe we could have lunch, or I could visit your room," he persisted. "I've been watching you."

With that, I turned and fled, unnerved by his disconcerting presence and perturbed by my utter lack of privacy. Thankfully, Connie had left our room for the cafeteria by the time I returned. Alone at last. Alone with my demons now set free to haunt my head with long-repressed memories, no longer held hostage by an intoxicated brain.

Control started to slip away when the children were born. Postpartum depression was not common talk in the 1940s, but after the birth of Beth, it swallowed me whole for a while.

Billy started his practice in northeast Arkansas. My family was not nearby, and I had no one to confide in. Of course, Billy knew something was dreadfully wrong, but he thought I'd eventually snap out of it. It wasn't something we talked about. We just lived with it. And therapy—well, therapy was for the mentally ill, and I definitely was not that. I was the pretty, young, small-town doctor's wife, who had just given birth to a beautiful baby girl. I should have been the happiest new mother on earth.

But a few weeks after Beth was born, I could not stop crying. Despair came in jagged, painful waves. The more the baby cried, the sadder and more resentful I became. It was no wonder she was such a fussy, malcontent child. My negative energy moved straight through her as I tried to comfort her the way I had seen other mothers do, imitating their holding and rocking, their cajoling. But for me it was forced; there was a void somehow. I wanted to feel a connection with my baby, and the fact that I was numb drove me even further into the web of depression. Sometimes, I just left her in the crib to cry. For how long, I'm not sure, but she learned to console herself. The way babies in orphanages do, I imagine. Eventually the crying stopped.

Bed became my solace and sleep, my bosom companion. Sleep was the surest way to escape the feeling of being tethered to this life. I craved it, lusted for it, got lost in my world of dreams—a world without crying infants, needy husbands, and sad mommas who weren't really cut out to be mommas.

I started drinking beer to facilitate the production of breast milk, a common practice in the day. Country doctors like Billy even recommended it. That was the real beginning of my undoing, when he began to make home brew in endless supply. It was another means of escape, numbing every cell, every damn, screaming cell. Drink a beer. Feed the baby, change the baby, put the baby to bed. Drink a beer. Climb back into cool, rumpled sheets. Disappear. Baby cries. Mom drinks a beer. The cycle begins again but whirs tighter, the centrifugal force rendering it impenetrable.

Then Billy hired some help for me—Byhalia—and she understood. Her kind eyes looked beyond my frailties and buoyed me with instant acceptance.

I'll never forget her first day. I had actually gotten dressed and bathed the baby, trying to make a good impression. It was the first time I had really looked in the mirror in days, and the image before me was dismaying—pasty skin, dark circles framing puffy eyes, wild hair. "Jesus," I whispered.

I heard her knock—she was a little early—and I threw a scarf around my head and slipped on sandals. "Be right there!" I scooped Beth up from a pallet on the floor and moved toward the door, awkward and unsure, as if my incompetence as a mother were in plain sight like an unsightly blemish in the middle of my forehead.

As Byhalia crossed the threshold all bright and sunshiny, pressed white dress against skin the color of fresh-ground coffee, an ethereal glow was cast by the morning light as it filtered through the muslin curtains. I could see her sizing me up, but not in a judgmental way. She wanted to help, and she moved fast. I could have sworn I caught a glimpse of a halo circling above her head.

"Miz Claire, how are you today?" she asked. Before I could answer, she went on, "I can see you need some help around here. No need to worry. Everyone needs help with a new baby. And I mean everybody. Especially a first baby. I know that's right," she said to herself as much as me, shaking her head dramatically back and forth.

She reached out her arms to Beth. "And look at this baby girl. Oh my, ain't she sweet?" A beautiful, toothless grin spread across Beth's face. Relief washed over me like spring rain.

"OK, Miz Claire. Why don't you go make yourself a beauty-shop appointment and do a little shopping today? Bet you haven't been out of this house two times since baby girl was born. You'll feel better. Don't worry, babies and me get along just fine. I'll just straighten up around here, too. Wash your sheets and such. Yes, baby girl and me gonna get along just fine, ain't we, sugar?"

Holding Beth like an extra appendage, she walked
over to the refrigerator and looked inside, surely mar-
veling at the lack of nutritionally sound food. "Mr. Billy
already gave me some grocery-shopping money, so I'll do
that in the morning and maybe fry up some chicken for
supper tomorrow night. How 'bout that? And make some
biscuits. I do make the best biscuits. They melt in your
mouth."

Her plans of what the days would hold were the sweetest sounds I had heard in a long, long time. Though my
demons lurked, the clouds lifted a bit that day.

ᖇ

"Claire. Claire, dear. It's about time for your session with
Dr. Kellogg."

Sissy's kind face beamed down, a bright-red headband
holding back a mass of blond curls from her smooth forehead. I had dozed off. Connie was curled up in the gray
vinyl recliner covered in a thin hospital blanket, book in
hand. She was smiling, too.

"Someone once said, 'sleep is like death without the
commitment,'" I offered dryly, easing up from the fog of
fitful dreams.

They both laughed.

"Ah, a sense of humor," Sissy quipped.

"Thought I'd lost it."

"A sense of humor is the next-to-the-last thing to go—
right before our hearing," Connie offered.

"What?" Sissy held a hand to her ear, feigning deafness.

"Ha-ha," I added with a wry smile.

Sissy nodded at Connie and inquired, "Were you able to get down any breakfast, Ms. Claire?"

"Haven't been able to try yet. I've always been partial to hot coffee first thing, but I can't even do that. I took a cup to the courtyard earlier, thought I'd try some, but the smell turns my stomach."

"That will get better. Your body is detoxifying. It's a beautiful thing, really. I can feel the good health coming back to you. How about I make you a cup of my special stash of herbal tea with honey? You can take it with you to therapy. It should actually settle your stomach."

"I'll try."

"Be back in a few."

I was nervous and jittery as therapy loomed. I slipped on my size-five shoes, and they were tight. Flesh bulged over the edges.

"Connie, you know the man with the crazy hair, the one who wanders around constantly? Do you think he's dangerous?"

"Harry? No, I think he's harmless. I've been in group therapy with him a time or two. He looks weirder than he is. He acts kind of shell-shocked."

"His name is Harry? Really?"

"That's kind of funny, isn't it? I'd like to cut his hair while he sleeps—like Samson in the Bible—or whoever that was. Harry's last name is something Italian. It starts with a T. Can't think of it … he overdosed, you know. Almost died. Said he felt responsible for his wife's death."

"How did she die?"

"Killed in a car accident. I think he was driving."

"Oh my goodness. Bless his heart." I suddenly saw the man in a whole different light. *Bless his heart indeed.*

Sissy returned, steaming cup in hand. "Special chamomile with calming herbs. Sure to cure what ails you. Now don't worry, Claire. Dr. Kellogg won't bite … much."

∽

"Let's begin with the first time you noticed that your addiction was out of control. Describe what was going on, what comes to mind, when you first felt fearful about losing control."

Dr. Kellogg seemed different that day, kinder, more empathetic, more human. His leather wingback chair was drawn close to mine. For the first time in a very long time, my shoulders came down a notch or two. I sipped Sissy's tea, took a deep breath, and steadied myself. I had never thought about his question—when I truly began to be afraid for myself, when I started losing control of it.

"My history is so long. How in the world do I pinpoint it?"

"Think about your awareness of the fear. When do you remember feeling most afraid?"

I took a deep breath, and a memory rushed in unannounced—or more specifically, it was my first non-memory.

"My first blackout. It would have to be my first blackout. I didn't remember a large span of time, and it scared the living daylights out of me."

"Good. *Good.* That makes perfect sense. Now, tell me what happened before and after the blackout, the events surrounding it, all that you can recall."

"It happened on a trip to New Orleans for Billy's annual American Medical Association conference. We stayed at the Hotel Monteleone on Royal, one of my favorites. Too many details?"

"Not at all," he said. "Details are key. Please continue."

"Good with the bad, I would imagine."

"Yes, of course. Remembering the good things is just as important as dealing with what hurts."

We sat in silence for a while as I conjured up the experience. It flooded back in all its misery. I felt a tear inching down one cheek and grabbed a Kleenex from the pastel box on the side table.

"Take me where you are, Claire."

"I remember everything leading up to the blackout very well. Martinis sitting at the Carousel Bar in the hotel. Billy was extra attentive. He hung onto my every word. But you know, it's curious. I remember watching the people around me. It was as though we were actors—not real life."

"Why do you feel you were acting? This was your life. It was real."

"I have no idea why I felt that way."

"Did you feel that way often with your husband?"

"Yes, I'm afraid I did."

"Can you tell me more?"

"I've felt that way about most everything for as long as I can remember."

"OK, then. We'll revisit that later. Let's get back to that day in New Orleans."

I paused with eyes closed, recalling the moment. "We walked to dinner, chatting, arm in arm. It was winter— we wore long coats. I can see the glow of gas lamps. We browsed in antique stores, and Billy gave coins to a street performer singing the blues. We stood and listened to him until we were chilled. Then dinner at Arnaud's—bottles of wine, cordials, I don't know what all.

"The next morning, Billy seemed on top of the world. He said something about a band and dancing. 'We should do that more,' he said. Then he told me that I had been wild, out of control, did things in bed—things I just didn't do.

"I could not believe what came out of his mouth—could not. I can hear him like it was yesterday. I panicked, but hid it. I had no memory *at all* after dinner. *Nothing.* Not dancing, not the bedroom, not anything. Billy left the room in search of a newspaper, and I ran straight to the toilet, hugged it, and retched until nothing was left. Before he returned, I managed to compose myself.

"I never told him that I'd lost most of that night. I was far too ashamed. Never again, I told myself. Never again would I lose time. But I broke that vow over and over."

"You felt it important to make that vow to yourself. Why?"

"Because once I start, I can't stop."

"Recognizing the inability to control yourself is a huge step, Claire, a crucial one. It's on the path to wellness."

"I'm really feeling ill." A wave of nausea hit me in the throat. "Need to lie down."

"Of course," he said, helping me from my chair. "Excellent first day. Excellent. Maybe next week you'll be up to a group session?"

"Impossible," I retorted. I wasn't about to go to "group" anything.

As he walked me back to my room, nausea ratcheted my insides again. I tried to bow behind a door before yellow stomach acid splattered on the floor tile and soiled the tops of his shoes. I felt too ill to even say I was sorry.

Once in the tiny bathroom of my cell, I cupped my hands and rinsed my mouth and face. The mirror did not lie. I had lost weight. They weighed me every day, but I knew it from the clothes hanging loosely on my skeleton. My eyes were sunken and my wrinkles pronounced without the puffiness brought on by binging. I looked like the shadow of death.

By this time Sissy had arrived with a dose of something to help. Uncharacteristically quiet, she intuitively knew what I needed and helped me under the sheets. I was unable to sleep; one bad memory brought to light the next in unforgiving waves of lurid lucidity.

One event from long ago was among these, ugly and true:

Billy and I had dropped Beth and Andy off at the movie theater on Main Street and said we'd pick them up when the film was over. Truth be told, we were happy to be rid of them for a couple hours.

Feeling free and celebratory, we started drinking the minute we walked through the back door. Billy put some jazz on the turntable—he loved Pete Fountain—and we became mellower by the minute, drinking and dancing to beat the band, not watching the clock.

Eight o'clock rolled around. Realizing in a panic that the kids' movie had ended almost an hour earlier, we jumped in the car, perfectly incapable of driving safely. Billy peeled out of the driveway, gravel flying in the wake. The theater was only five blocks away, but we were too stupid to walk.

Billy was in worse shape than me that evening, unaware that he was unaware. He stormed into the theater to retrieve the children, bellowing their names. I trailed behind, too drunk to be embarrassed. Then I caught sight of them huddled in a corner under the staircase to the balcony. Beth's arm was circled protectively around her brother. The sight snapped me out of my stupor.

"I don't want to get in the car with him," Beth whispered to me under her breath.

A gangly teenage couple stood nearby, mouths gaping.

Billy heard Beth's words and stormed out of the theater. He walked home.

"Is Daddy mad at me?" she asked, confused, after he left.

"No, honey. No. It's OK." I put my arm around her and patted her, then put the other arm around Andy. "Daddy just had a little too much to drink tonight. You know he can be a little loud after he's been drinking."

The car keys were in Billy's pocket, so the children and I walked home, too. I tried to make up for the scene with small talk about the movie. The next morning, we all acted as though nothing had happened. Beth even hugged her daddy at breakfast, but little Andy stared absently into his oatmeal, stirring but not eating.

The look on my young son's face that distant morning told the story, and it has haunted me since. It was the same look when he reminded me of my promise to go to rehab. I sobbed myself to sleep that night with the wrenching recollection and realization of my little boy being raised by an alcoholic Pandora. *Bless his heart ...*

∽

Going through the motions in purgatory the next day, in a semifunctional state of catatonic compliance, emotionally numb from the nightmare that was my life, I "woke up" in therapy when Dr. Kellogg confronted me with a question from the previous session. He remembered what I had said about "acting" at life, not feeling it was real much of the time with Billy. "Why?" he wanted to know.

"Because I was in love with someone else." The answer popped out as if Sissy had laced my hot tea with truth serum.

"Ah. *Ah.* That is crucial. Who was it that you were in love with, Claire?"

So I told him about Henry, about my soul finding its one true mate and then losing him, and about my life after his death:

After losing Henry, I could not let go and *just be* in the world again. I held onto my grief and pain frantically, obsessively, like it was the only way to keep him alive. This colored everything. Oh, I faked it at times, smiled, laughed, engaged—even married Billy after a few years. But down deep, I wanted to be where Henry was. Period.

As quickly as possible after the funeral, I'd dropped out of college and boarded a train bound for home. I had to distance myself from Georgia. What else could I do? My heart was hemorrhaging in my chest cavity, drowning in hot crimson. I cried constantly, even though a sense of Henry being nearby was visceral at times. Although I never saw him in a vision, I would wake in the night and feel him, skin to skin, the way we slept, limbs twined around limbs, feet touching. Henry's spirit tried to comfort me, I believe, but I wasn't ready. I couldn't get past the question, *Why, God damn it? Why?*

I remember his funeral. There was standing room only in the simple Methodist sanctuary, stark and Puritan, whitewash and wood as dark as the devil. Droves of people encircled the front door, shocked and bewildered by the unfairness and randomness of it all. Funerals of the young always bring people out of the woodwork, even those who had only a cursory relationship with the deceased. Maybe they needed to see to believe. Or maybe it was a necessary exercise of coming face-to-face with the fragility of life, the impending, rapidly encroaching mortality of each and every one of us. Maybe it was simply morbid curiosity, like feeling compelled to look at the aftermath of a fatal accident or the charred remains of a house fire. Our relationship with death determines so much about life.

I sat among Henry's siblings, as did Morgan and Tony, his best friends and hunting buddies. They were never the same after the accident, either, especially Tony. I heard he never forgave himself, took his own life ten years later after a long bout of abusing antianxiety drugs. Shot himself in the chest with a shotgun. Used a screwdriver to reach the trigger.

We all wore dark glasses and huddled together, trying en masse to keep Henry's mother afloat, fragile creature that she was. Friends offered what must have been poignant and inspiring eulogies, but I couldn't hear a word over the deafening roar in my head, an echo of the grief screaming in my heart. Nor do I remember the drive to the cemetery, just a lingering image of his gladiola-covered casket being lowered into the red Georgia clay.

I will never forget the day Henry asked me to marry him. Never. We had spent the night at his cabin on the family farm, a retreat set amid venerable cedar and oak, a pristine spring-fed creek within earshot. The morning was cool, and Henry built a crackling fire in the pit outside. As I walked from the cabin to join him, a blanket around my shoulders, I noticed an uncharacteristically serious look on his face.

"Come sit by me, sweetheart," he said, patting the camp chair beside him.

"What is it, baby? What's wrong?"

"Oh, nothing's wrong, nothing at all. I just have something to ask you."

I was not expecting a proposal at that moment. Someday, yes, but he caught me completely by surprise.

"I love you very much."

"I love you, too."

"I want to spend the rest of my life with you—more than anything. I hope you feel the same way." There were tears in his eyes. I had never seen tears in his eyes. "I'm asking you to marry me."

"Oh my God, yes! The answer is yes!" Our embrace at that moment was filled with such spontaneous joy that we both cried and kissed softly in the loamy woods. "It has always been yes."

He knelt beside me, took my hand in the gentlest way imaginable, and pressed lips against my skin, hot and soft. Then he looked up at me and slipped a ring that had belonged to his grandmother on my finger. It fit perfectly.

The seeds of addiction were always there. Maybe this is so for every one of us—kernels of destruction sown in fertile psyches that seek escape from the ever-present internal dialogue, the constant battle between the self we are impersonating and the self we wish to be.

My husband, William Danner—Billy—entered my orbit shortly after I dropped out of college and returned to Tennessee. He was a close friend of my older brother, James, from their days at Sewanee, and they came home for the weekend after my return from Georgia, especially for the myriad festivities planned by Mother.

A busty Irish woman just under five feet tall—and sadly, I didn't inherit the large-bosom gene—Mother was in perpetual motion. She was known far and wide as the quintessential hostess, and everyone who was anyone in Hardin County and beyond coveted an invitation to anything she cooked up. You'd think I was a new debutante the way she was divining. Maybe Mother thought she could wrap a blanket of activity around my loss and coddle it away. She was trying, God love her, to distract me from myself.

My welcome back was a huge garden supper, an event I dreaded. I simply wanted to be left alone to disappear into the musty fabric of my childhood bedroom. But Mother was insistent, and I did make an appearance at the soiree in a loose, black dress hung on a thin frame, with an anti-social expression on my wan face.

"I'm doing this for you," she reminded me, slapping my derriere.

Billy and my brother, James, were eligible bachelors in the thick of establishing careers by then. James had landed in Knoxville working in finance, like Daddy. Every girl in town vied for his attention that weekend, especially my best friend, Hildegard. I believe she'd lusted after that boy from the day she was born. I accused her for years of being my friend only so she could be near James. He looked at her like a little sister, though. Always had.

James was so very handsome and as charismatic as my Henry. They'd met on one occasion—James and Henry—and took an immediate liking to one another. James had come to Atlanta to visit a young lady he was seeing, and the four of us had great fun dancing until the wee hours. James was, of course, as shocked and saddened as anyone to learn of Henry's death. Even my friends who didn't know Henry grieved at the grim news. I surely wished Mother and Daddy could have known him. They'd have been more patient and understanding, I think, instead of expecting me to snap right out of it.

That night at Mother's garden party, sweet Billy sought me and sought me. He didn't push; he just sort of began the process of pulling me in. Tall, rail thin, and blond, he was the antithesis of my dark-haired Henry in many ways—quiet rather than gregarious, serious where Henry was jovial. I think it helped that Billy was so different. I saw him through a completely different lens.

I was terrible company at that point, a veritable vegetable, spending my time staring glassy-eyed out the window or holding a book in my lap pretending to read. Daddy's whiskey became a warm crutch at night to ensure coma-like sleep. When the house was quiet for the night, I'd tiptoe downstairs to the ample liquor cabinet tucked away in a low corner of the library, the familiar decorative key dangling from a chain on an intricately carved door. One side of the room had wide windows and sometimes a view of the moon. I would curl up in a worn velvet chair, nightgown tucked under my feet, and take tiny sips of whiskey from the bottle while dreaming of Henry. His touch, his smell, his laugh, the way it felt with his manhood inside me, hot and beautiful and right. Sometimes I'd slip my hand under my gown and pleasure myself, fantasizing that Henry's spirit was right there watching. Smiling. Then the energy between us would get too intense, and he'd return to mortal form just to make love to me. Or so I'd imagine.

I tried to project my mind to where he was. I tried to connect with his spirit, what essence was left. *Are you on the moon, Henry? The silvery moon? Are you lighting up the sky with your giant aura? Are you with God yet? What is my lesson here? What am I to learn? Please tell me. What is the good to come of this? Everything happens for a reason. That's what everyone says. There must be a Goddamn reason!*

I began the pattern of anesthetizing myself. Without my nightly toddy, sleep became as elusive as a phantom, no matter how bone tired or gravelly eyed I was. Sleep ran from my reach, slipped away and left me cold.

Over time, Henry's presence became less palpable. I no longer felt him in the same way. I speculated that at first he was between worlds, held in this dimension in part by my suffering. A time came, though, when it was right to become enveloped in the light and for him to transition to heaven. It was a comfort to imagine him there, but it did nothing to squelch the deep, persistent ache of his absence. Nothing did. Well, Daddy's whiskey did. It softened the frayed edges.

Why Billy was so taken with a dark, sullen girl like me, who was not in the least bit interested in a relationship, I will never understand. He surely was the most patient, persistent man alive. He wrote me letter upon letter. After six months, I agreed to cocktails at the local hotel bar. Eighteen months later we were married at Calvary Episcopal in Memphis—a halfway point between our family home in

Savannah and Billy's in Arkansas—in a ceremony that was casual for the day.

The dramatic downtown sanctuary needed no embellishment, though. And the atmosphere that fall afternoon was warm and loving with a web of immediate family and close friends gathered to send us on into our new life. Mother had carried champagne and wedding cake, nuts and mints, all the way from Savannah, bless her heart. My wedding attire was an ivory silk douppioni suit and pillbox hat. Billy told me I was the most beautiful creature he had ever seen. He would never be able to *see* me the way Henry did, nor I him.

I hoped for the best, but to be truthful, doubts hovered underneath my veneer of wedding cheer.

My parents had fallen into a financial abyss and were basically without the means to support a lifestyle of the sort we had all grown accustomed. I didn't know this until my return home. Daddy had made some unwise investments and put a second mortgage on our home—we didn't lose it in the end, thank God. I wasn't privy to any more details. Didn't ask, didn't want to know. They were surely relieved to see me marry and lessen the financial drain. And they knew of Billy's family—felt we were a right-good match.

We honeymooned in Saint Louis and consummated our marriage. I learned that Billy was a heavy drinker, too, and we fed off of one another's momentum once we got started; neither of us minded. I guess everyone has demons he or she wants to dumb down, or maybe just a bent to convert fun into compulsive habit, for lack of something more compelling to affix one's attention.

But I felt profoundly alone in those years, as if the wind could blow right through me. I felt empty—the best parts of me scooped out, a brittle and hollow shell left behind. Billy's easy manner and convivial company became a balm. He made me laugh like no one else could at that point, and he adored me. And I was drawn to his family without reserve. They were prominent landowners and close-knit, even clannish.

Billy grew on me. Like scotch, he was an acquired taste, and I could see myself as part of the tribe, wife of a young doctor. Maybe accepting a little bit of living was OK. Maybe being Henry's martyr was not all that was in store. Billy knew my story and loved me anyway.

Grace: First Love

The day our family took Mama Claire to rehab, my sister, Elizabeth, and I decided to whip up some margaritas to cut the tension and celebrate my return from south of the border. We had the house to ourselves.

As Elizabeth juiced a dozen limes, I sat on the kitchen counter beside her, recounting my newfound sexuality with Javier. Four years older, Elizabeth was experienced in that way—she had already done the deed with five guys. *Five!*

"So, do tell, Gracie." She couldn't wait to hear. "Tell big sister *all* about it."

"OK. First let me say this: Oh. My. God. He began—our very first time, mind you—by licking and sucking me down there." I pointed to the crotch of my jeans and grinned. "My first orgasm was with his mouth. His beautiful, beautiful mouth."

"Wow. *Wow.* No kidding! How old is this Javier? I've actually never had anyone do that."

"Twenty-eight."

"A real man then. You started with a real man. Who knew you had it in you? Way to go. I guess I've only been fucked by boys. Maybe that's the problem. I think we need a shot of tequila on that one. Wow, Sis."

We poured two shots and clinked the glasses together before downing them.

"To oral sex," she toasted with mock seriousness. "Or more specifically, cunnilingus ... isn't that the correct term?"

"Cunnilingus. The word sounds so fucked up, doesn't it? But I'll drink to it."

"So, how'd you meet him?"

"Well, he's the son of my host parents. My host mother was the most amazing cook. And she even let me help her—taught me real Mexican cooking. I'll have to cook for you some night."

"You cook? Seriously?" She laughed. We both laughed. "OK. You digress. Please get back on track with the good part."

"Well, he joined us for dinner one night and stayed— told his parents he was sleepy from too much wine. During dinner I could feel his eyes burning into me. He has this energy—I can't explain it. Every time our eyes met, my heart skipped a beat. *God.* And knowing he was going to be under the same roof all night ... I was naked under the sheets fantasizing about what his lips would feel like when I heard a quiet knock on the door. My room was on the other side of the hacienda from the other bedrooms, so we were virtually alone."

"More!"

"I'm not telling you more. You are so perverted. You've always been like that."

"I absolutely am not!" Elizabeth exclaimed in mock indignation, manicured hands on slim hips.

"Yes, you are quite seriously perverted, and everyone knows it!"

"Who knows it?"

"Our family, your close friends ..."

"Shut up."

"No one likes to talk about sex more than you. Just go curl up with one of your trashy, pornographic novels, Sister, 'cause I'm finished. No mas."

Elizabeth threw her head back and laughed languidly, and returned to the duty of stirring up the margaritas as if it were drudgery. Her small form seemed deflated at the thought that I was finished with my tale, but it was probably an act to spur me on. Elizabeth was manipulative like that. And it usually worked.

"OK. Don't pout. I'll tell you more, just not the down-and-dirty stuff. That's not even the best part. Don't you want to know how I feel about it all ... if I love him? If he is *the one*?"

"Well, is he?" she asked as she poured the icy concoction into salt-rimmed glasses and handed one to me. Her smile was open, sincere.

"Let's take these outside," I told her. "I really need to talk this through."

The day was overcast, the air heavy, reflecting the gravity of the day, the intervention with Mama Claire, now on her way to confinement in a rehab hospital. And I was feeling pangs of longing. I missed Javier. Elizabeth and I curled up in lounge chairs and took tart sips, not talking for a while underneath the low dingy clouds. A warm buzz began to kick in from the tequila shots. It had been eons since we made time to catch up, with me in college and Elizabeth busy with her first real job in marketing at a regional bank.

"How does anyone know—I mean know absolutely for sure—who is *Mr. Right*? So much about Javier felt right. But if I even have to ask the question, does that mean the answer is really no?"

She turned toward me, her head resting on the nylon cushion. "You know, I want to believe that when you meet the right person, that's it. No questions. You feel it in your marrow ... in your freaking marrow."

"Yeah, me, too. You think that actually happens?"

"Maybe, if you're lucky. I don't know, since it hasn't really happened to me. I thought I loved Jason. Remember him? Jason Jones?"

"That was a long time ago. Your senior year in high school, right?"

"Yeah, senior-year loss of my innocence." Elizabeth made a dramatic face, and we both laughed.

"Jason was your first?"

"I think that's why I thought I loved him. I must have loved him—right—to give it up to him? Why else would I open myself up? I think that's the way most girls think. We rationalize."

"Maybe so."

"My infatuation with Jason lasted about a year. Then his clinginess got so tiresome. And I was leaving for college. I can still see his face when I broke it off. Jesus, I hurt him. But it was the right time."

"The path of love is never smooth, I guess."

"So, how do you feel now that you're away from Javier? Was it only that one night?"

"God, no. We were together at some point every day after that. He runs an art gallery during the day—he's an artist, too—but his work is sculpture made out of found materials. Way cool. You'd love it. So I had class until two each day; then I'd hang out at his gallery and help. At the end of the day, we'd lock the door and make love on the couch in the break room. Then dinner. Then make love some more … we could not get enough."

"You are glowing, Sis, talking about him."

"Am I?"

"Like a slow-burning flame."

Like a slow-burning flame, yes, I was still burning for him, embers smoldering in my heart, hot coals in my erogenous zones. I missed his smile, his long fingers on my skin, his manhood unlocking the secrets of my femininity, the scent of me intermingling with his must. Was it lust? Was lust enough? Our beat-up old outdoor cat jumped up on my chaise and curled up between my legs.

"So, what was it like when you said good-bye?"

"Sad, really. I didn't want to leave. I felt at home in San Miguel. But I only knew him a few weeks. I couldn't change the whole trajectory of my life, could I? My last year of college is coming up."

"People do it all the time."

"Not in our family."

"Well, yeah."

Javier had already called several times since my return home, talked of a visit to the States. What would become of us, I couldn't say. But we connected, so much so that it scared the hell out of me. I wasn't sure I wanted to be so tied to one person so soon in life. If it was meant to be, it would be, I thought. I missed him, though. Deeply.

Claire: Buried Secrets

"Good morning, Claire. How do you feel today?" Dr. Kellogg was intent. "We dug up a few old bones yesterday, did we not?"

"Yes, and those old bones haunted me all night—wouldn't let me be. I think we should leave the rest of them right where they are. They've been down there a long time."

Dr. Kellogg nodded slowly and began to finger a smooth rock on his desk, a beautiful piece that looked as though it had been polished by eons of rushing water.

"We can see the past in this rock, many years of a stream carving and smoothing it into the shape we see today. Our past is like that in a way. What streams through our mind for years, what we've carried with us from our past, creates much of who we are today and will be tomorrow. This occurs mostly without us really realizing it. If we want or need to change who we are, we need to look back, look within, and see what's still shaping our lives, our thoughts. Claire, it's necessary to dig, but please understand, it's not merely to reconstruct and relive old hurts and old mistakes. That would just be punishment, and this is not about punishment. We're going through this in order to take the old bones out of the grave and into the light just long enough to make peace with them, and then put them back where they belong, for good. Is any of this making sense to you?"

I looked down and nodded. "But what if I don't really care about changing who I am? What if I'm sick and tired of this life and just too damn old to change?"

"Claire, no one here or anywhere can force you to change or to do anything you really don't want to do. You are here and have made it this far because you're not ready to die. If you were, you would have already taken your life. You were not dragged here in leg irons or a straightjacket, so you must have agreed to give it a try. You must have had enough love still left for your family to at least humor them. The issue now is not your love for them but your love for yourself, which is the most essential element.

"Claire, I know this is difficult for you right now. Please trust me when I tell you that what you're going through is very normal and absolutely necessary if you want to recover your true self, the one you were born with, the life given to you as a gift from God to be filled with the joy of learning and loving. The person that is hurting now is not the real you. See this person as someone to observe. Be the witness. The real you is that part that will still be around after you leave your body behind. The real Claire is the one observing the pain, directing the scene, and not the pain itself. Sometimes we become lost in what we are thinking and feeling."

I looked up and searched Dr. Kellogg's eyes. "I understand what you're trying to do. Lord knows I do. But I can't help feeling that my life is over, that there's too much water under this old bridge to be worth the trouble to repair it."

"Try to consider the possibility that time is not a factor. Consider the possibility that each of our lives, every single moment, is a special and unique expression of God's creation, with infinite potential. Consider the possibility that you are here and that all you have experienced was and continues to be absolutely appropriate for the evolution of your soul. Consider the possibility that the very act of your recovery, the act of forgiveness, is why all this messy and painful past was created in the first place. Consider that this moment—you and me right now digging up the old bones—is an important part of your personal journey into a more expanded and complete human experience."

"I think it all sounds a bit farfetched, but I admit this isn't the psychobabble I expected. There's a feeling of truth here. Even so, I'm just not sure I can continue. I'm really tired."

"Will you try something for me? Will you repeat something for me?"

"Do I have a choice?"

"Always."

After a long pause, I sighed, long and deep. "Dr. Kellogg, I don't see much harm in hanging in there a bit longer to see where this goes. Maybe the real Claire is lurking in here somewhere and wants to be set free. I surely hope so."

"OK then. Repeat after me: I forgive myself for all my mistakes … I did the best I could for who I was at the time …"

Dr. Kellogg then led me through a series of forgiveness statements, essentially designed, he said, to give me "a tool and a catalyst for self-forgiveness." Reciting them felt hollow and meaningless, but he tried to assure me that our words have the power to create our reality and that I should trust in this process and keep doing it, even if I still felt like my same old self. It all sounded too good to become true, but I had begun to trust him and his intentions, even though I was unsure of his methods.

∽

The next day, Dr. Kellogg was especially chipper. "Good morning, Claire. Did you do your releasing and self-forgiveness statements since our last visit?"

"To tell you the truth, I'm having a hard time with this. It doesn't ring true. How can I expect to erase a lifetime of regrets by simply reciting a few sentences?"

"You must give it time. It's the story we tell ourselves that determines who we are. If we want to change our story, we have to start telling a new one, even as the old one continues to play in our head and in our hearts. Please believe me that words, repeated with the right intention and integrity, have the power to create a new story. Just do it, please. Trust me on this."

"OK, OK, I'll try."

"Thank you, Claire." Dr. Kellogg paused, closed his eyes in what seemed a silent prayer, and then added, "Today, I'd like for us to talk about your relationship with your children. Beth and Andy, correct?"

"Yes. Beth and Andy."

"How do you feel your addiction affected them?"

"*Gravely.*" My lower right eyelid began to twitch.

He nodded and pressed one finger into his temple. "I know this is difficult, Claire, likely the most difficult to face."

I dreaded this line of inquiry the most. How had my irresponsible behavior affected my beautiful children? The thought resurrected a stabbing pain in my chest. I closed my eyes and tried to take myself there, but I couldn't. Another memory began to take shape, a nightmare I had repressed for over forty years. *Another child? My God. It was our baby! My lost baby!*

I curled over into my lap, becoming fetal—the pain too much, unable to speak. I could only cry. I remember Dr. Kellogg trying to comfort me. Then nothing.

෭ඉ

I awoke disoriented, unable to focus. Sissy told me I'd been asleep almost twenty-four hours—that I'd been sedated. She bent down and kissed my forehead. She smelled of clean hair and lilac.

"Welcome back, Ms. Claire. I have orders to call Dr. Kellogg as soon as you wake up."

"No. No. Please don't call him."

My tongue was thick, my mind groggy from sedation. I struggled to remember what had happened.

"I must follow Doctor's orders, dear." Sissy nodded to her assistant, who immediately disappeared.

Dr. Kellogg materialized and sat at the edge of my bed. He took my hand and smiled warmly. "How are you doing, Claire?"

"Like a hangover from hell."

"That's understandable."

"What happened to me?"

"We'll catch up to that later. Today is a day of rest. I've already instructed Sissy's assistant to bring meals to your room."

"*Please.* I need to know what happened. *Please.*"

A rush of adrenaline-laden anxiety began to clear away some of the cobwebs, and a flash of my breakdown in therapy came back.

"Very well." He took a deep breath and massaged my hand as he spoke. "Claire, the extreme stress of reliving a long-repressed memory contributed to what we call a brief psychotic disorder. This is common, no need to worry. It is actually positive, I believe—a breakthrough."

It rolled over me then, the feeling of losing the baby. Henry's baby. *Our* baby. Hot tears streamed down my cheeks.

"I remember. *I remember.*"

൭

In the wee hours, I was awakened by another nightmare, but this time it was not mine. Guttural moans and the words "no, no, noooo" pulled me from my restless slumber. Where the hell was I?

I sat upright and saw Connie in the dim glow, her body thrashing, her face stony with pain, eyes tight shut. My instinct was to go to her, and I did. I tried to hold her hand, to place my hand over her heart. At first she fought me and almost knocked me off the bed.

"Connie, it's all right. Wake up, dear."

"Don't touch me, you motherfucker. Ever." She tried to slap me and missed. Her eyes were still closed. She was dreaming.

"It's me. Claire."

I shook her gently, and she began to come out of it. She sat up on one elbow, her nightgown plastered to her sweaty body.

"I dreamed it again. Fuck. I dreamed it again. Why? Why?"

She rolled over and sobbed into her pillow. I rubbed her back, not sure what to say or do. Finally her body began to quiet, and her breath no longer came in gulps.

"How can I help, honey? Want to talk?"

"It's too awful. I can't."

"I've lived long enough to have seen all kinds of awful. I know what it feels like to push awful so deep that you think it's gone. But eventually it creeps back in. Some of mine did yesterday."

"That why they sedated you?"

"I'm afraid so."

She sat upright and hung her head. Her hair fringed around her face like a raggedy curtain. "It feels like if I speak it, it makes it true."

"What's true? Do you want me to call Sissy or Dr. Kellogg?"

"No, please don't call anyone. I can't talk about it." She fell back onto the bed again and pressed the pillow over her head.

"Let it out, dear; let it out if you can. I'll never tell another soul."

"It's why my life's been so fucked up," she told me from underneath the pillow. "Why I'm here."

"Then it's high time to let it go. What happened to you is not who you really are." Such spontaneous parroting of Dr. Kellogg surprised me. I was listening after all.

Connie pulled the pillow away and searched my eyes, looking for trust. She then pulled herself up and shuffled to the bathroom. I heard her empty her bladder and flush. When she returned she had put on a robe and pulled her hair back into a ponytail. As she began to speak, her countenance changed, as if an insidious being possessed her narrative. A chill ran through me.

"He began coming to my room at about age ten—my dad. He waited until Mama left for work at her night job. I remember it as clearly as you and I are sitting here right now."

Her arms were crossed tightly, and her fingernails dug into freckled flesh.

"I was almost asleep, and I felt him sit down on the edge of my bed. 'How 'bout I rub your back, Princess? Would that feel nice?' I rolled to my side and found his face in the darkness. His big hand was hot like fire. He rubbed my shoulders first; then he worked his way down. He ran his hand under my panties and over my bottom and snaked it down my thighs. At first it felt nice. Then he spread my cheeks and touched the inside of my bottom. I heard him sort of groan—like an animal. That's when I got scared.

"'Daddy, what are you doing?' I remember saying that. I rose up and wanted to run.

"'Only daddies can touch girls here,' he told me. 'No one else. It's special, Princess. Just between you and me. Always.'

"I wasn't sure if it was true. It felt flat wrong. But maybe it was true, I thought. My daddy wouldn't lie to me.

"He told me to roll over on my back. I did what I was told. He hiked up my nightgown and slipped off my panties. He licked his finger and stuck it into me, into a void that I didn't even know was there. It hurt bad.

"'You'll get used to it,' he told me. I was shaking like a leaf. When he left the room, I was afraid to open my eyes. I squeezed them tight and pretended it never happened until the next time he came. He didn't actually penetrate me until a few months later. I thought I would die."

Connie had been in a trance as she spoke, but her eyes met mine then, gauging my reaction. Tears flowed down my cheeks. No words of consolation seemed enough.

"My dad fucked me and fucked me every chance he got, so much so that it began to feel normal. I was isolated, had no real friends. At fifteen I became pregnant with his child. But it wasn't real to me. I was close to my second trimester before the signs were unmistakable—couldn't keep a thing down. But somehow I hid it from Mama. Then good ol' Dad took me for an abortion and told the doctor right in front of me that I had gotten knocked up by my boyfriend. They sucked the fetus right out of me. That was that. I felt ruined, a freak. The clinic gave me birth-control pills so it wouldn't happen again. I ran away a year later—stole enough money from Mama's purse—hopped a bus for El Paso. Spent some time in Mexico. Stayed high, mostly."

"Oh, honey." I took her in my arms and rocked slowly. She caved her emaciated form into my body. At first she didn't cry. She just shook. Every muscle trembled.

Her words jarred me to the core, a saga horrific to the point of being unimaginable. The very fact that she was sitting next to me beating an addiction, with hope for the future, caused something inside of me to snap loose.

As bad as my story was, it seemed a trifle compared to what Connie had just unleashed. As I held her and felt her sobbing release come in waves through the night, an unbreakable bond formed. Throughout what would remain of my life, I had acquired a sister, a surrogate sibling discovered on the climb from the abyss. We both turned a corner that fitful and cathartic night.

꩜

Billy came to visit the next day. I was not ready. I did not have the right words for this good man. He deserved so much more.

It felt so strange seeing him, as if he had invaded my private hell, a place I never wanted him or anyone else to go. I didn't want him to see me all naked and vulnerable without my usual armor of anesthetization. I didn't want to struggle to make small talk. I didn't want to talk about the past. I didn't want to hurt him anymore, either. I loved him for so many reasons.

And a disturbing feeling kept coming back—a gnawing guilt about marrying Billy in the first place. It was something that I *let* happen instead of wanting it or choosing it. It was mindlessly selfish; he deserved better. He deserved someone who adored him the way he adored me. Maybe after so many years he was so accustomed to the one-sidedness that he didn't even notice.

How to make amends? Lord in heaven, I had so many to make. And I was feeling my stage of life, the fleeting nature of time, the winter, if you will, of my earthly existence. Maybe I had just enough time to do some good.

"Claire, my love."

I stood as he entered the room, and he took me into the familiar fold of his arms. I felt his love. I smelled his smell. He pulled back and kissed my cheek.

"Oh, Billy. I am so sorry for all of this."

"Now, now. It's all going to be OK."

Billy stayed the full hour allowed and didn't push me to talk. Didn't push me, period. I was glad he'd come after all.

After he left I thought about how he'd lovingly enabled me to be a drunk. He'd done the best he could at the time.

Billy's visit triggered a memory. I let myself feel it, relive it:

It was the end of a regular day. I heard Billy's car roar up the driveway. He always drove like a bat launched from hell. I hadn't thought about my appearance or what we might have for dinner, so I scurried to my vanity for a lipstick and put a brush through my hair. I smelled my underarms. Had I bathed? Who knew?

It was a game we played, Billy and I. He pretended not to notice most of the time and even brought booze and food so I wouldn't get in the car. He understood. For years we drank too much together, spending afternoons making love and then passing out. Even after our children were born, we lost days until his medical practice began to suffer. So, on his fortieth birthday, he made the decision to quit. There was no conversation about it; he just never drank another drop. Cold turkey, as they say.

But Billy took care of me. He knew I'd stop if I could. And anyway, it was none of anyone else's damn business.

"How was your day, honey?" I said as he came through the door. He carried a bucket of Kentucky Fried Chicken in one hand and his briefcase in the other.

"Long. Not particularly bad, but long. The needs of the unwell are never ending," he said, meeting my eyes and knowing everything without asking. He smiled—not in a carefree way but with the compassion of many shared trials, many shared years. I'd take that smile, though. It was what kept me going.

"Anything interesting today?" he asked.

"No, it was quiet, really. I did a lot of reading. Caught up on some correspondence."

He pulled me close, reached down, and cupped my ass in his hands. "God, you feel good," he said. "Let's have some chicken."

Grace: Dark Shadows

I used to sit with Mama Claire and pore over her scrapbook, a monolithic epitaph to another time, a carefully crafted collage of a life. She was so proud to show me the mementos—ticket stubs, programs from plays where she was the star, photos of sorority life as a Tri Delta. There were handwritten notes from suitors, her word for her old boyfriends. Her stories seemed to jump off the page, and I never saw her more animated than when she was reliving that time.

She was the dark-haired beauty in the perfect frock, winner of scholarly awards, a college girl at a time when college girls were a rarity. She danced and partied with the most-eligible young men in New York City, Atlanta, Saint Louis, Nashville, and Chicago. As she traveled from city to city, new contacts forged and the invitations poured in.

Indeed, she was a beauty contestant representing Tennessee in the Fairest of the Fair contest at the 1932 World's Fair. She wrote to her mother on stationary from her perch in Chicago. Her handwriting, so familiar to me from birthday cards and notes of support over the years, elegantly sprawled across time-yellowed stationary from the Drake Hotel:

Mother Dear,

This is the very first chance I've had to write you, and there is so much to tell you that I don't know where to start.

When we got here Friday we were taken straight to Marshall Fields and had fittings and a welcome lunch there. Lucy B. and I went out after Fields, and we talked a good while. We didn't even get to our hotel until one o'clock that night, and we were dead! Then the next day we had more fittings in the morning and at noon had lunch in some swanky room in Marshall Fields. It was terribly exciting because we had to parade our white-and-red dresses, and there were oodles of people on all the balconies watching us eat. Then that afternoon, Friday, we had the judging, which was impressive and lovely. In fact, all our chaperones said that they had tears in their eyes. The judges tried to make it as easy for us as possible—and Mother, the girl who got crowned queen certainly deserved it. She is the most-perfect-looking creature I have ever seen.

That night we went to the Sherman Hotel and had the coronation. And then yesterday, Saturday, we had the parade. It lasted an hour and a half, and I never hope to see so many people again. Honestly, it was like pictures we have seen of Lindberg coming home—there were papers flying and everything.

I'm rooming with Ida Rittenberg, a girl from New Orleans. She's a Jew but such a lovely girl. And I'm crazy about our chaperone. We have had the best time in the world, and I wouldn't take anything in the world for the trip. Of course, we are half-dead because we go every minute of the day and night. I haven't even had a chance to call Lucy again, but I will today.

Will you meet me in Memphis on the way home?

I haven't time to write any more now. Give my love to all the family and lots to you.

Claire

P.S. Lester M. called, and Dick Taylor keeps writing and calling! I have an afternoon and dinner date tomorrow with Wood Griffin—set up by Lucy, of course!

Mama Claire's letters to her mother were testaments to the fact that she was being groomed for a young titan, and my great-grandmother was a co-conspirator. She'd have lunch at "the club" with one beau, cocktails with the "right" group, then dinner and dancing with yet another crowd of eligible young men. Each date seemed to be a notch in her proverbial belt, and she felt the need to relay the details to her mother, as if it all were a game. They were keeping score; someone would be the victor and she, the prize.

But somewhere amid this fabulous ruckus, she returned to her hometown for a visit and met my grandfather, a plainspoken gentleman with deep Arkansas roots and modest aspirations, very different from the up-and-coming captains of industry and privilege described in her letters. At that point the scrapbook stops. Something happened. Quite possibly the crucial pieces of my grandmother's puzzle.

Maybe she was in love with Pop, romanticized life with him but crashed emotionally under the burden of unrealistic expectations. I don't know. She was a debutante, by God. There were certain things she felt she deserved, that she was entitled to, that became lost in the mundane world of a small Delta town in Arkansas.

77

Curiously, I never heard her speak of her wedding—not once. No wedding album, no fairy-tale story. And my mother had not been born in the first year of marriage either, so this was not a marriage of necessity.

Who were you, Claire Steadman Danner? Who were you, so full of promise and hope for a time, only to spend a good portion of your life trying to disappear? What happened?

∽

All the recent drama surrounding my beloved grandmother being forced into rehab made me think quite a bit about her, who she was and who she became. These musings triggered my continued self-examination of periodic alcohol abuse. What were my rationalizations and pressures, insecurities and demons, which pulled me down that same dangerous path? What did I want my life to look like? And why was it I, and not my mother, daughter of the drinker, who succumbed? Why did I crave it from such a young age?

I grew up with a healthy fear of drugs—well, what I considered *real* drugs like cocaine and weed and prescription pills. I was afraid of anything that might make me lose control, or of having some kind of unforeseen, unknowable trip. I should have been afraid of alcohol, but who thinks of family history as a teenager?

I did, inadvertently, take serious drugs once. I have no idea what it was, but it was wicked.

It was my sixteenth New Year's Eve, a party hosted by college guys looking for prey, and I was handed a drink that must have been laced with something. I only have flashes of memory, but each image is one I wish to forget.

The day began with the delicious anticipation of taboo. My mom would never have approved of the party, which made it all the more enticing. My best friend, Sally, and I told her that we planned to visit several parties that night.

"Where exactly are these parties?" Mom wanted to know. There ensued vague descriptions and circular talk intended to throw her off the true scent, a technique that usually worked. A name dropped here, a party location there, possibly we would meet at a restaurant. Neil and Sam were going, too. She loved them and thought they were "good" boys. Mom could be a pretty soft touch.

Elizabeth inquired about our plans—that she approved was a most dangerous sign—and proceeded to give the following sage advice: "Don't eat too much so the drinks will go straight to your head." She was brilliant at age twenty.

We entered the cavernous din of a rambling ranch house. Parents absent, Pink Floyd in the background, and a drink placed in my hand before I could even take off my coat. I remember being initially flattered by the attention.

The main den of excess was a large room set several feet lower than the rest of the house, with black leather furniture, chrome lighting, and ivory-colored shag carpet. Couples were already sprawled out on the couches beginning to make out. I was tingly and excited by this very adult scene. Moans could be heard from behind closed doors as couples moved to privacy to be more intimate.

I downed the drink, and the next thing I recall I was facedown on a strange bathroom floor. I rolled over, and distorted-looking faces peered down, studying me like a science project.

"Who is that?" someone said. "She looks fucked up."

My name echoed off the sea of green tile on which I was marooned. My mind told my body to get up, but a disconnect somewhere kept me prone on the cold hardness. I remember wondering about Sally. Where the hell was she? When would she come and rescue me? I desperately wanted to go home. I vomited and fell back into the sea.

I awoke on a bed this time with an unknown boy kissing my lips, my cheeks, my ears, my neck. The sensation was not unpleasant, so I closed my eyes and was still. Then he began to press his body on top of mine with an urgency that alarmed my few remaining cognizant cells. I was clothed, thank God. I remember moaning, "No, no, no, *no...*"

Sally walked in at that moment and pushed him off me. I was aware enough to be really grateful. I'm still grateful. She drove me home, somehow half walked, half carried me to the front door, propped me up, and gave me to my mother.

"Sorry, Mrs. Banks," she said. "I really don't know what happened." I remember her saying that. I was actually sick for days after. I still wonder what the hell I ingested.

We are all addicts, really, aren't we? Slaves to something? And isn't it natural to want to partake of all this majestic world has to offer? The plethora of grandeur—whether it be the view from atop a mountain, the endless turquoise sea below, or ingesting a drug that will enhance our senses and loosen the barriers of inhibition? We all want to revel in the richness. But where to stop? If something is enjoyable, at what point does it become compulsion? At what point does it begin to cause problems and pain? When is enough, enough? Maybe it all depends on the impact it has on others, or on one's own health and ability to function in the world? Maybe Mama Claire somewhere crossed the line without knowing it? Maybe you just know it when you see it. Maybe you don't.

∽

Mary Hannah Dixon called and said she was organizing a Rhodes girls' weekend before classes started.

"My parents are in Europe! We'll have the place to ourselves!"

"Nice," I told her. "I'm definitely in."

I'd actually lived part of my junior year of undergrad in the Dixons' pool house, a luxurious little suite nestled behind one of the most beautiful homes on Central Avenue. It was Mary Hannah's idea—I'm not sure where she came up with it—and the arrangement sweetly evolved.

Mom had driven over and lunched with the ever-so-glamorous Dixie Dee Dixon at Paulette's in Overton Square. Mrs. Dixon assured Mom that they "just loved me to pieces" and thought it was a wonderful idea for me to live there and get out of that "dreadful dorm." She also said I was a good influence on Mary Hannah in the grades department. Little did she know I had not been so great an influence in other departments, such as the partying department.

After much discussion, my parents finally said yes. Mary Hannah and I jumped around and screamed like thirteen-year-olds.

On the way to that crazy party weekend at Mary Hannah's, I decided to stop and see Mama Claire at rehab. I had been worrying about her constantly. It was week three of her stay, and family visits were allowed.

As I drove the forty miles from my hometown to the rehab clinic, a conversation I'd had with Mom the night before kept circling around in my mind. We had stayed up late talking about everything: my trip to San Miguel, as well as a new project Mom had brewing—what would be our town's first secondhand store for the poor. And we talked at length about Mama Claire and how she was progressing at Greenleaf.

"What was it like, Mom, growing up in that house?" I asked that evening. "I mean, Pop drank, too, for a while, didn't he?"

"He did, yes. But it's hard to put into words, Grace, what it was like. Maybe if I tried to write it—get my feelings down that way—I could come closer. Uncle Andy has had all kinds of therapy through the years, and maybe that's better. I've relied on prayer, some pastoral counseling, and mainly your dad. He has been my rock and so, so patient. God knows I was a mess in my twenties. I cried all the time. I was trying to be newly married and a mother, all while trying to live in the same town as my mother and continue to deal with her issues."

"I guess I've taken it for granted that you've always been, you know, so together as my mother, my source of inspiration and strength for as long as I can remember. It's hard to imagine you being a mess."

"Thank you, sweetie."

"If you don't mind talking about it, I really want to understand."

"You sure you want to know?"

"I already know enough to *need* to know. Remember, I lived some of it myself."

"Well, there is one day that stands out in an indelible way. It marked me for better or worse."

She took a sip of Pinot Noir and sighed. "Let's go out-side and look for the moon. Tonight is the blue moon. We can talk out there."

"Wonderful."

Mom spread a quilt across the grass in the backyard. The night was soft and wet, expectant.

"There. What do you say? Perfect?"

"Yes."

Our view of the moon was unobstructed and exquisite, a giant, luminous orb carefully placed in that spot by God's own hands. We were silent for a while, meditating without trying.

I looked over at Mom and was captivated by her beauty in that light. She truly looked youthful, the photons of moonlight magically dancing away the years. The blue moon pulled at my soul, love tugs, and whispered in my ear that everything is good and everything changes.

"Still want to hear an old, depressing memory?"

"I do."

"OK."

I still felt hesitance from Mom. Now I know why. "You don't have to tell me if you don't want to."

"No. No. It's OK." Mom paused and gazed past the moon as she began her story. "We got off the bus at the corner one block from home like any other day. I was eight, Andy, five. He had just started kindergarten and was the cutest little boy you have ever seen—dark-brown curls, brown eyes like Mother's.

"We walked in the door expecting Byhalia and cookies and milk. But instead the mess from breakfast and lunch was strewn all over the kitchen. I even noticed some empty beer cans. I yelled for Mother, but there was no answer. We bounded up the stairs, innocent as lambs."

Mom looked at me. Her eyes welled. My heart beat faster.

"Their naked bodies were twined up in the bed linens, and they didn't move. I walked over to Mother's side of the bed and shook her, but she just groaned and babbled a string of incoherent syllables that ended with something about finding Byhalia. Her mouth was slack, her eyes closed as she spoke. I took Andy by the hand and led him downstairs to the kitchen. He whined about being hungry—seemed oblivious to all the ugliness. Maybe it was his way of dealing with it all."

"God, Mom. That's terrible."

"I remember trying to distract him, trying to sound grown-up—'Let's just take a nice walk to Miss Juanita's and have a hamburger and a malt. What do you say? It will be an adventure, Andy, I promise. You stay right here, and I'll run up and get some money out of Daddy's billfold.'

"So I ran up the stairs and scanned the room for the billfold. The light was dim, the shades drawn. I had to step over a blue dress and black lace panties to reach the bill-fold on the dresser, surrounded by loose change.

"I remember wondering how much hamburgers cost. And I remember hating them for the first time at that moment."

"Oh, Mom, I'm so sorry you lived through that, and Uncle Andy."

"It's OK, sweetie. It was a long, long time ago. One thing struck me, though, while I was telling you the story. In my heart, I became responsible for Andy that day. I had suddenly become a little adult. I took him to Juanita's Café—it was about six blocks away—we ate hamburgers and ice cream and pretended everything was fine. When we got home, they were still passed out, but the covers were pulled around them, thank God. I made sure Andy had a bath and brushed his teeth. That was the first night I ever prayed."

∽

The Greenleaf Rehabilitation Center was *the* most depressing place I'd ever been in my entire life.

We humans have compounds where we sequester people who don't fit in—rehab centers, psych wards, prisons. I wonder, though, if this is designed for the benefit of the folks with problems or more for the rest of us, who prefer to keep the misfits out of sight and out of mind?

When I walked through the door, the first thing I noticed was the people—patients, I assumed. They eyed me skeptically, warily, like I could somehow be a threat, all 115 pounds of me. I guess I looked lost because a nurse intercepted me and asked if she could help. Her face was so open and familiar, like we had met before.

"I'm here to see Claire Danner, my grandmother."

"Well, I see the resemblance. You're both so beautiful. I just happen to be Mrs. Danner's nurse. My name is Sissy O'Brien. Come with me." She took me lightly by the crook of the arm.

"How is she doing?" I asked as we walked down a fluorescent corridor.

"Much better. Really well, in fact. She's something special, you know."

"I know."

"I've learned as much from her as she's learned from me."

"I believe that."

We walked into Mama Claire's room, but she was not there. I was struck by her little stark room and bed, such a contrast to her beautiful bedroom at home with her antique dark-walnut furnishings, white linens, cozy fireplace, and large bay window with a view of an expansive green lawn punctuated by stately, century-old trees.

"I'll bet she's in the library or the courtyard," Sissy said. "That's where she usually hangs out."

There wasn't a soul in the library, so Nurse O'Brien led me through a maze of identical hallways to the courtyard. I could see Mama Claire on a bench in one corner visiting with a rail-thin, middle-aged woman.

Mama Claire glanced my way, and she beamed. Her arms opened wide as we walked toward her.

"Grace Anne," she said. "Oh, honey, I'm so happy to see you! This just makes my day."

We hugged like it had been years. "Connie, this is my granddaughter. You probably gathered that." Mama Claire was actually giggling.

I nodded to Connie. "Pleased to meet you."

"Same here. Claire really sings your praises."

After some polite small talk, Connie and Sissy left us to ourselves. I sat with Mama Claire on the courtyard bench where Sissy and I had found her, apparently the only private place in the whole compound.

"So, tell me about Mexico. How was it? How is everything?"

She took my hands in hers and massaged them with her bony thumbs. She had lost weight. And I noticed for the first time a striking similarity in the size of our hands and finger length, the way our nails grew, the shape of the tips. But the likeness gave way to age—smooth skin versus mottled age spots; bulbous veins instead of hidden ones; prominent, bony knuckles and knuckles nestled in young flesh.

"Well, I hate to talk about me. I came here to see about you."

"I'm moving along, Grace. Opening up, coming to grips with myself, letting go of some old, old baggage. It's been hard ... but *necessary.*"

I nodded emphatically.

"It's been like waking from a long, bad dream. I must relive all that my mind will allow. Realize the pain my behavior has caused others. *And* forgive myself. That is the absolute hardest part—forgiving myself. I am not there yet."

"Can I ask you something?"

"Of course, anything."

"I've always wondered why, Mama Claire. What happened? Is it all right for me to ask that? It seems like you had so much to live for. I'm asking for another reason, too, because I sometimes feel like I have a problem with control myself."

She looked away. The memories still evoked emotion after so many decades.

"Well, there's no pat answer, no simple reason for anything, you know? Life can be complicated. But if I were to boil it down, my trouble really began when I lost Henry. His name was Henry."

"Who was Henry?" I was surprised by this revelation.

"Henry and I met when I was about your age, and it was love at first sight. We were engaged to be married and planned to spend our lives together." A visible shudder went through her. "He was the other half of me, Grace. That's the only way I can explain it. We were connected in a way that I have not known since. I hope that doesn't sound wrong to you, since I spent the better part of my life with your pop. I do love Pop, you know. He has been wonderful to me. Better than I deserve."

"I know you love Pop. It's OK. I'm old enough now to understand. What you've told me is beautiful. So what happened with you and Henry?"

Claire studied the wrinkles on her hands, worrying her wedding rings back and forth.

"He died in a hunting accident after we had been together almost a year. I thought my life was over. I did a damn good job of drinking most of it away, didn't I? I dropped out of college and hightailed it home."

"That's terrible!"

"Oh, there's more. And I've never told another soul this except my psychiatrist here. When Henry died I was pregnant, but I didn't know it. My periods were never regular; they just surprised me now and then. A couple of weeks after I was back home, I began to spot. The next day the most terrible cramps doubled me over, and I took to the bed. I guess the stress of Henry dying and perhaps my drinking made me lose our tiny boy. I've blamed myself for the baby's death my entire life. Maybe I thought I could have dealt with the stress better someway.

"I passed him in my childhood bed, all alone. He fit in the palm of my hand, a perfectly formed little creature. I remember staring at him and rocking him, unable to believe it, unable to cry. When he was cold, I wrapped him up in a towel and headed straight to the woods behind our house to the edge of Caney Creek. I was very weak and bleeding heavily. I folded a hand towel in my panties to catch it all."

She sighed, long and deep, and I noticed that her hands shook as she painted the picture. Tears dripped from my cheeks.

"When I got to the most beautiful spot by the creek, at the foot of a giant cypress tree, I dug a hole with sticks in the wet dirt near the water. I unfolded the towel and gazed at him, studied him for what must have been ages so I'd never, *ever* forget. I reached under my hair and unclasped my cross necklace and draped it over his body, then swaddled him and placed him in the ground and covered the grave with dirt and soft, green moss. I curled up beside him and cried until dark came and Daddy's voice echoed through the trees, calling me home. I didn't want to leave him or leave that place. I wanted to die right then and there, to sink into the earth with him. Then we could all three be together.

"That secret has been buried in me since that day. Until I came here and everything was unearthed."

I envisioned the scene and tried to imagine how Mama Claire must have felt—how I would have felt if I were her. But I couldn't imagine anything so awful, hoped I'd never have to. We sat holding hands in silence for a long time, each of us in deep contemplation.

Good God, I thought. *Good God.* But I felt special in a way. She trusted me enough to share her darkest hours, to say the words out loud. My Mama Claire. God bless her.

෬

I was completely spent when I reached my car. The visit had not at all been what I expected. It was powerful and heart wrenching; it rocked me. Parts of me felt expanded, like I had absorbed some of Mama Claire's hard-earned wisdom through osmosis. But unfortunately, my common sense wasn't a beneficiary, because my first inclination was to get a drink. Boy, did I need a drink. Plus, I was on my way to a party!

During late high school years and college, my modus operandi had devolved to the following: if I was upset or nervous before a test, about to go out on a date, or if it was anywhere near the weekend, a libation was in order. You name it, and I could come up with a reason to have a drink.

A cooler full of beer and wine coolers called to me from the trunk of my car—my contribution to Mary Hannah's party. I downed an icy wine cooler and grabbed another to sip on while I drove.

A slow drizzle began to fog my windshield and pool on the hot asphalt as the lazy warmth of alcohol hit my bloodstream. Ah, sweet relief!

I merged onto Highway 63 and headed toward Memphis, overjoyed to be leaving small-town Arkansas and all that it entailed and demanded. Fumbling to find a Steve Miller Band cassette, I spilled my second wine cooler in my lap. In a blink, a red pickup appeared from nowhere, horn blaring, tires screeching. Instinctively, I jerked the steering wheel and stood on my Mustang's brake pedal. Then everything went black.

Claire: Resolutions

A random memory came to me at supper that night after Grace's visit. The cafeteria had served some pretty awful strawberry shortcake for dessert—sugar-laden, gelatinous strawberries on a stale Twinkie. The thought of fresh strawberries brought back the spring of 1967, or maybe it was '68:

"Miz Claire, Thursday is bridge-club day. Don't forget. You is the hostess. What you want for dessert this time? Any idea?"

"How about strawberry shortcake, Byhalia? The strawberries are so perfect right now, and everyone loves your little shortbreads. They are the most buttery, divine things I've ever put in my mouth."

"That's fine, just fine. I'll go to Piggly Wiggly tomorrow and make it fresh."

I had a new dress I was saving for bridge club. On the day of, I spent the morning picking irises in the yard and arranging them, all the while nipping at a bottle of wine stowed in the back of the refrigerator, as if I could hide anything from Byhalia. I'd refill my glass when she was out of the kitchen, then steal away to the backyard and false privacy. By noon, I'd consumed the entire bottle.

I hadn't had a drink in two weeks, having resolved to stay sober for Beth's surprise thirtieth birthday party at the country club the weekend prior. I could temporarily abstain if I felt strongly enough about the reason. That was the thing. Usually I didn't feel strong enough to wait until noon to get started. Most days were like that.

Although my children seemed to be doing well as we crept into our fifties, Billy was more distant, stayed away more, hunted more, played more poker. My gut told me he was having an affair—with whom I hadn't a clue. Frankly, I didn't care that much. Sex was the very last thing on my mind. I was dosing myself heavily the vast majority of the time. I couldn't blame him. *Work late, please,* I thought. *Let someone else take care of those never-ending needs.*

On the morning of bridge club, I was inexplicably weak. By one o'clock, an hour before the arrival of my guests, I was far enough gone that I had also downed a double highball of scotch while I bathed. I got out of the bath, hardly drying off, and climbed between my beloved sheets. By that point I didn't have a care in the world. I had begun to disappear.

Byhalia knocked on the door, a few gentle raps.

"Byhalia, I beg you, please go away." I pulled the covers up high and covered my face with a satin pillow.

"I can't. I wish I could. It's only an hour till they come, Miz Claire. Only an hour."

She cracked open the door and peeked in.

"Miz Claire, *my law,* what have you gone and done?" She walked over and stood over me. Of course, I reeked. "You gone and drunk too much. *Lordy,* what am I going to tell your friends?"

"I don't care what you tell them. Please shut the door."

It was too late to call the guests, and Byhalia did not know who all was invited anyway. When the ladies arrived, she told them one by one in a most contrite voice, "Miz

Claire is sick in bed. I'm sure sorry." I am positive Byhalia felt enough shame for both of us.

ᘓᓓ

Connie joined me at the supper table. I was glad to see her. As we sipped weak iced tea flavored with a packet of lemon concentrate, the conversation eventually got around to the subject of addiction. It usually did.

"It's the best high in the whole world," she told me matter-of-factly. "Nothing like it."

We were unlikely friends. It was the sort of companionship that springs from the shallow rocks of institutionalization. I had asked her about the grip of meth—what it was about the drug that had held her so tightly. We had moved way beyond small talk, and her spirit and intelligence shone like warm lights.

"I'm telling you, Claire. I've tried everything. You name it. Meth is different. Cocaine doesn't compare. The world looks clearer, more alive, full of promise, or at least you think it does. Fears are gone. Energy surges through your veins like wildfire. You stay awake for days, every nerve standing on end. You believe anything is possible."

She shook her head incredulously. "I'm not sure exactly what it does to the brain, but it is a fucking fabulous, out-of-this-world high. If I could do it now without repercussions, I'd do it. I'd just stay high."

She tilted her head back and closed her eyes, no doubt reliving the rush. A sigh emanated from her bony chest. She turned to me with eyes set too deep in their sockets and smiled, sad and crooked. "But it will kill you—snuff you right out. The good part of you disappears behind a dark side that only cares about getting high. You will lie, cheat, steal to get it, by God, and nothing else matters. In the end, you lose everything. So, I'm lucky, right? To be where I am?"

"We both are, honey. We both are lucky to have this chance to come out the other side, whatever that means. I believe that now, or at least wish for it. But sometimes I still ask myself why the bad things had to happen. Why did I stay so lost—waste so much of my life? Is it too late to start over?"

Connie looked down at her hands, massaging the V-shaped spot between the thumb and forefinger firmly, one side and then the other, and added, "For me, I felt completely alone and lost after I ran away from home. I tried to fill this hole in my heart with whatever I could get my hands on—usually a loser guy. I was like a giant infant gobbling up everything around me, greedy but empty. So, I searched in all the wrong places, over and over, almost destroyed my health, alienated everyone. And here I am, looking for a good reason to stay straight, still looking for a reason for living in this crazy world."

"I understand the need to find a good reason to keep on trying. It would be easier to let go of this life and be free—just free. And truthfully, I don't know if I can make it in the real world without a drink in my hand. I will say this, though: I believe I'm here, with you and Sissy and Dr. Kellogg, for a reason. I'm beginning to feel connected again to this life and the people in it, even though it hurts like hell sometimes. But at least I'm able to feel the hurt—the love—instead of just going through the motions half-dead and drunk."

Connie nodded slowly in agreement and after a pause said, "I just have one question."

"What's that?"

There was a playful twinkle in Connie's eyes. "If we're all suppose to be here to serve others, then what are all those others here for?"

I could not contain a smile. I loved her like a sister.

Connie then raised her glass of tea in the air as to make a toast. "Here's to another round."

"Here, here!"

We clinked glasses and giggled like schoolgirls.

"What should we do tomorrow? A facial? A full-body exfoliation and massage?"

"I say manicure and pedicure, with mimosas on the side." Connie pretended to soak her nails in her half-empty cafeteria tray.

We both laughed.

"The champagne would get us both into trouble," I said feigning a frown. "We'll have to keep that out of our fantasy. I've had enough champagne in my day to float the Titanic."

Suddenly, I saw Sissy stride with purpose through the doors of the cafeteria, straight to our table. Her jaw was set, her expression serious.

"Claire." She took my hand. "There's been an accident. It's Grace."

"Oh, dear Lord, no …"

A tsunami of shock thundered through me, an uncomfortably familiar blow. I pushed myself up from the table and felt my knees buckle. Sissy bolstered me under the arms.

"Claire, the doctors think she's going to be OK, but she was in a very serious accident after she left here today—crossed into the path of a truck. They're still evaluating her condition."

"Tell me everything, Sissy, *everything.*"

"I don't have many details. My conversation with Beth was very brief. She and Tom arrived at Saint Bernard's Hospital about an hour ago. Billy's on his way. My friend Robert Van Dyke is taking care of her. He's an excellent trauma specialist. She's in good hands, Claire. I will not leave your side until we know more."

"I want see her. I need to be with her."

"No one can be with her yet. It's still too early. And I'll have to talk with Dr. Kellogg to get permission for you to leave right now. It's protocol."

"To hell with protocol. I *must* see Grace."

⤜⤛

Rain was coming down in sheets by the time Sissy and I left for the hospital. Dr. Kellogg had given special permission and said he knew it was vital that I go. But I felt a bit like I had escaped from prison with Sissy as my guard. I vowed that day that as long as I lived, I would no longer be in a situation where I needed permission to see my grandbaby. I would no longer wallow in my putrid vat of despair. No more.

The emergency waiting room was fairly empty, except for one unkempt couple with a sickly looking infant whose hollow eyes followed us as we rounded a corner. Then I saw Beth, her husband, Tom, and my Billy.

Beth wept audibly as I took her in my arms. Sissy and I both cried with her.

"She's going to be OK, Mother. They say she's going to be OK."

"I know, I know. Of course she will."

I could feel my daughter tremble from the trauma as I hugged her. She pulled back and smiled a haggard smile. A sweet, young nurse brought a tray of coffees, and we all sat heavily.

"She was unconscious, briefly. Her head hit the driver's-side window," Beth told us. "There was some slight bleeding in her brain, but not enough to require surgery, and the doctors don't expect any brain damage, *thank God*. She's conscious now, but sedated."

"Well, thank the good Lord."

"She broke her collarbone, a few ribs, her left femur, and some bones in her left foot, but nothing that won't heal over time," Beth continued. "She was extremely lucky; she wasn't wearing her seat belt."

Tom sat with his elbows resting on his knees, his eyes studying the floor below him. One hand seemed to be bracing the other to control a slight tremor. Reticent by nature, Tom was quiet and let Beth tell the story.

"Oh, and she'll have to have surgery on her leg and foot. We're not sure when, though."

"Tell me about the accident, Beth. What in the world happened?"

"Grace crossed into the path of a pickup. Looks like it was her fault. The driver of the truck is in intensive care, too—has a wife and small children. The police who worked the accident said if the truck had been traveling at full speed, or if they had hit fully head-on, neither one would have survived."

"Oh, my Lord. Have you seen her?"

"Yes, briefly," Tom interjected. "Her left eye is swollen completely shut, Claire. Really the whole left side of her face … I don't want you to be too upset when you see her."

"I need to see her, just for a few minutes, to pray with her. She'll hear me."

☙

Grace looked like a wisp of a child swallowed up into the white expanse of her intensive-care hospital bed. Machines beeped and hummed around her. The acrid aroma of Betadine filled my nostrils. A few lovely auburn tendrils of hair escaped beneath the bandages, the only sure sign of her except for her lips and chin, which appeared untouched by the trauma.

Oh Lord in heaven, lift Grace Anne up to you on wings. Please mend her body and spirit. Please allow me more time on this earth with this precious one. Please give me strength to set aside my shame and guilt and become a source of love and inspiration for Grace and all those I love. Amen.

I cupped her hand in mine.

"Grace, honey, it's Mama Claire. I'm here. I love you with all my heart. You are going to be fine. *Just fine.*"

Her eyes were shut, but she squeezed back. It took all that I had to choke back a cry of joy and release.

God is here, I thought, *just as sure as my heartbeat.* The room was full of Spirit. I began to feel what they had been telling me about recovery being more likely if one can surrender to a higher power. I began to see the old tapestry of my life fade and a fresh canvas emerge. Peace spread through my center, the kind they talk about that "passeth all understanding." It was the first time in many years, since Henry died, that I felt God was real and alive and there for me, too.

꩜

As we turned into our longtime neighborhood, emotions wrought from the perfect sameness of every simple thing flooded through me—Myrtle's porch covered in a menagerie of cats, John Thomas waxing his old Dodge Charger for the ten-thousandth time, the natural beauty of next-door neighbor Susie Wright's carefully tended landscaping, the majestic old magnolia tree on the corner where Beth and Andy built forts under the wide canopy. There was my own front door, deep crimson with a brass knocker the shape of a heart. Billy put his key in the lock, and I watched for the familiar crinkles around his eyes as he turned to me and smiled. I was home.

The week after Grace's accident was my last week in rehab—the end of the twenty-eight days. Connie would stay another month before the stubborn tentacles of her issues began to fully unwind. Our good-bye was not a good-bye at all. It was a beginning.

I would miss Sissy's pure spirit and positive energy, the persistent way she pushed me toward myself, a path that I had shied away from for decades. Miraculously, she believed strongly enough for both of us. Why she believed in me I would never completely fathom. When we parted, I told her that her God-given gifts were being used most perfectly. She replied that patients like me made it all worthwhile. Just the thought of her still makes me smile.

Once settled, my one suitcase tucked in the bedroom closet, I filled our battered teakettle and lit an eye on the stove, the *snap-snap-snap* of the lighter yielding to a soft whoosh from a circle of blue flame.

"Earl Grey or spiced tea, dear?"

"Earl Grey, please, ma'am," Billy answered as he filled the bowl of his pipe with a pointer finger and sat at our old gate-leg kitchen table, his long legs stretched straight out, loafers crossed at the ankles. A new normal hovered around us, creating its own field of energy.

"What has it been like for you, Billy, with all this time and space to think?"

"The loneliest time I can ever remember."

"Even lonelier than all those years when I wasn't really here?"

"No doubt about it. I'd rather have half of you than none of you."

"You mean it?"

Billy propped his smoldering pipe in the ashtray and eased up from the table. I felt his hands and arms surround my form from behind and pull me gently into his perfume cloud of pipe tobacco. He lightly kissed under the back of my ear, sending tingles down my neck and between my shoulders.

His warmth humbled me. I felt a deep gratitude—for him, for God all around us, for every little thing. Taking care not to break his caress, I retrieved from the cabinet two matching china cups from a set that had belonged to my mother, feeling at that moment connected to her and a legion of souls stretched across time and space.

I turned around in his arms and searched his eyes. "Can you ever forgive me, Billy? Truly?"

"There's nothing to forgive."

"Do you believe we can put all this behind us?" I asked, knowing he would reassure me.

"It's going to be the best time of our lives."

A knock at the kitchen door made us both turn to see the pensive faces of our grown children through the panes.

"Come on in, you two." I motioned to them. "Door's unlocked."

"Mother, we're so thankful to have you home," Beth gushed as she pulled me close. "So thankful."

Andy put his arms around the two of us, tears in his eyes. "I'll echo that thought," he said warmly. "Love you, Mother."

I needed my family's forgiveness, and by all account it appeared they did indeed forgive my many years of being absent—or worse. It occurred to me that they needed it as much, if not more, than me. An epiphany. As ironic as it seemed, the greater benefit inured to the one doing the forgiving, the one releasing the anger, the one taking control of his or her equanimity and letting the past slide back into the past. This truth made me all the more thankful to see their faces full of relief and love without any traceable signs of resentment.

They inspired me to face the deeper issue still pricking persistently at my heart, which was my need to forgive myself, to decide that I deserved another chance after all the misery I had facilitated. No more going through the motions. No more being lost in a dream of what should have been, might have been, and would never be.

Henry was smiling. I could feel it. I could feel from him the same sigh of relief I saw now in Billy's eyes.

"Beth, Andy, I have something to tell you."

"Yes, Mother?" they said, almost in unison.

"I want to thank you for taking me to rehab. I know how difficult it was. It was the most courageous and loving thing I think anyone has ever done for me. I love you both very, very much. Now I have a chance to prove it to you."

"I left something in the car; I'll be right back," blurted Andy as he disappeared through the back door.

Beth's eyes followed her brother, and she spoke to fill the silence. "Oh, Mother, I don't know quite what to say … I'm so happy you're back, and healthy again. We were so worried about you."

I searched Beth's eyes. "Honey, there are not enough words in the English language to express how I feel, how ashamed I am for everything I put you through. I want you to know how proud I am of you, so proud of how responsible and caring you've always been, so thankful for you."

Billy pulled Beth gently to his side with one of his long arms, and catching my eye, nodded at the back door.

"Maybe you need to check on Andy."

I found him leaning over his car, both hands on the front fender. He had been crying. I knew he didn't want me to see him that way, but there was so much I wanted to tell my son, so much I wished I could undo. He looked my way, eyes red and wet.

"I'm sorry," he said, and wiped his eyes with the back of his hands. "I really can't explain why I'm crying. It's so good to see you well and seeming so … I'm not sure how to feel. I've been angry for so long."

"You have every right to be angry, and I don't blame you, Son. Let's face it: I have not been a good mother. Beth and Byhalia took better care of you than I did. There's nothing I can say that will change that now. All I can ask and hope for is that you will find it in your heart to forgive me."

"Of course I forgive you. It's just … well … are you really cured? Or is this just another hiatus that will end one day without any warning? And if you are cured, then why didn't you do this before now? I'm sorry … I guess I'm … I don't know."

"Andy, I honestly cannot tell you for sure that I'm cured, that I will never drink again. Only time will tell. What I can tell you for sure is that right now, as we're speaking, staying sober is what I want the most, more than anything else in the world. I believe I'm at a place in my life where that's really possible, more so than any other time before."

I took his hand, and he responded by clasping both his hands around mine; and our eyes, the same deep-brown pools, reflected upon each other eons of humans searching for balance and meaning, as well as for a renewal of the primordial connection between mother and child, something denied this child his whole life. He must have felt something similar, because the response was more than I could have hoped for. My son then put his arms around me and pulled me close, as two souls reconnected for the first time since the umbilical cord was literally cut.

"I love you, Mother."

"I love you, too."

Grace: The Unbroken Circle

I missed the fall semester at Rhodes that year. I was busy recovering—and growing up fast.

A wheelchair was my transportation at first, then months on crutches. My underarms were practically calloused. I was back in my old bedroom at Mom and Dad's for almost five months, back to dependency. Rehab, rehab, and more rehab for my left leg and foot. I spent so much time with my physical therapist that I began to have a crush on him. Just a situational crush—nothing with staying power.

Seeing your life pass before your eyes changes you. I took less for granted and appreciated the small things more. That sounds cliché, but truth is truth.

And I will always be dealing with the fact that a man's life was altered forever by my mistake, my recklessness. His name is Brent Jones, and he didn't ask for me to crash into him. I visited him at home—he wasn't able to return to work for nine months after the accident. His head injury was quite serious, in a coma for several weeks, and his short-term memory was affected. He didn't even know his wife at first, I was told. I was full of regret and guilt and needed to come to terms with what I had done, look him in the eyes and apologize, even though a mere apology could never make amends. Nothing could.

Brent's house sat solitary on a gravel road, and I felt profoundly alone as I made my way up to that front porch, still on crutches, my knees practically knocking. His wife opened the door before I reached it, as if she expected trouble.

"Who are you?" she asked.

"I'm Grace Banks, the one responsible for your husband's accident."

"What do you want with us? Haven't you done enough?"

"I just wanted to apologize to you and your husband, in person."

The woman paused and looked somewhere beyond me. The furrow between her brows ran deep as her emotions. A tiny girl with pigtails pushed between her legs and looked up at me with a smile.

"Come on in," she said with a tone of resignation. "Brent's in here."

The place was dark, small to the point of being claustrophobic. Brent Jones was rooted into a recliner, a television as large as the living room wall blared as he sipped something from an oversized plastic cup. As he turned to see me, his face registered surprise. An angry scar hovered over one eye, visible proof of my sins.

"Brent, this here's the girl who crashed into you." She left the room as she made my introduction. It was the last time I saw her. The tiny girl clamored at my feet, eager for any attention. My heartbeat was surely visible through the thin cotton of my shirt. Sweat dripped from my armpits.

"Mr. Jones, I don't really know what to say except that I'm so sorry for what happened. So, so sorry."

His eyes softened a bit, and he shifted in the recliner, reached for the remote and muted the volume on the NASCAR race he was watching. He didn't say anything for what seemed like half an hour. Just looked at me, studied me. When he did speak, it startled me.

"Girl, we've all made mistakes—every last one of us. I don't hold it against you. God knows I wish it hadn't happened, but all we can do is go from here. I appreciate you coming all the way out here to see me. Shows what you're made of."

A confluence of emotions that would take years to untangle washed over me as I negotiated the dusty path that led away from a family, a scene, a set of circumstances that I wished to God I could forget. But I would never forget that day, the faces, the emotions, the meagerness of the surroundings, the very tension in the air from my presence. Most importantly, though, was the realization that everything we do or neglect to do has a consequence. Nothing can be undone. For one fact, however, I was grateful. Brent Jones survived and had the chance to live the full monty again. I did, too.

I wasn't sure if Brent knew the truth—that I had some alcohol in my system when we collided. My blood alcohol level was under the legal limit for a DWI, but I remember feeling it, the loose carelessness of the drug. A policeman visited my hospital room once I was conscious, pointed out the potential consequences had I tested higher. His words made me feel like a piece of shit, and I appreciated that. I cried the rest of that day and into the night. It was a huge turning point. All of it was.

When the winter semester rolled around, I was thankful beyond words to be back at my beautiful little college with its massive trees towering naked in leafless wonder. I stood that first day, looked straight through the branches into the crystalline sky, and appreciated the storybook quality of the Gothic architecture, fresh faces, the energy of purpose, crunchy frost on the grass, the smell of cold. Everything in my life seemed renewed, vibrant, and inspired.

Dad had spent the weekend moving me back into the Dixon's pool house, and it felt good to be in Memphis again, where my soul felt at home. It was like I had my own place—a loaded kitchen, great electronics, and a Jacuzzi for a bath, which was good for the pain and stiffness on the left side of my body. I still limped a bit, but no complaining. I was alive. And what's more, I felt alive.

Mary Hannah spent the first night with me in my reclaimed digs. We curled up, cozy like sisters, and talked until two or three in the morning.

"I'm not the same as I was," I told her. "Never will be."

We were lying on our backs in bed, looking at stars through the huge skylight in the ceiling.

"How did it change you, Gee? Describe it."

"Well, I can't drink anymore; that's clear. I had to be literally whacked in the head to realize it, though.

"But mostly, I think more about what really matters— love, relationships, making a difference in some way, how I want to live my life. I can't even imagine partying like I used to party."

"That's too bad," she said, giggling. "You were so much fun. Now you sound so old and wise and boring." She turned on her side and looked at me with sea-green eyes framed in dark lashes. She made a pouty face and pinched me with her toes. "You know I'm kidding. I'm with you—*I am*. I'm rethinking a lot of things, too. Like how often I've gotten behind the wheel—not just after a few drinks, but completely wasted.

"The night of your wreck, we all waited around for you, drinking rum punch like fish and dancing quasi-naked around the pool."

I laughed, thinking of all my Chi Omega sisters drunk and half-naked.

"Seriously?"

"Yeah, seriously. But I kept wondering where you were. I couldn't get you off my mind. For one thing, you're never late. You're the only person I know who's never late. Finally, your mom called. She was at the hospital and told me what happened. We were all in complete shock—sobered up *real* quick. But we weren't in any shape to make the drive to Jonesboro. None of us. That's why I didn't come till the next day."

"That's cool. I was out of it for a few days anyway. I don't remember anyone coming that first week."

"I did come. Every day for a while."

"I know. Mom told me. You're the best."

"I got to know your grandmother—wouldn't trade anything for that."

"She's the best, too. I'm so lucky in so many ways."

"Were you scared when it happened? Or did it all happen too fast?"

"I vaguely remember seeing the truck coming toward me. It seems like I saw the driver's face, but that's probably a dream. It felt like my heart stopped just before the crash. I thought I saw death."

"Geez Louise."

"Yeah."

"Death is so final," Mary Hannah mused, worry knitting her brow.

"But it's not. What I saw and felt after the crash is hard to describe, and I'm still trying to understand it. I saw light. I felt the most unbelievable love. I saw my Mom's nanny, Byhalia, and she told me to look after Mama Claire. I guess it was like one of those near-death experiences you hear about. It was just … just not the same as dreaming; it felt real. *I* was there. Anyway, I woke up believing that death is not the end."

"Wow. Hope you're right, Gee. What a wake-up call—right?"

"For true. I don't ever want another one."

"Hey, how's your leg? Long day hobbling around campus?"

"Yeah. It still aches, but it's so much better than it was."

"Want me to rub it?"

"I love you, Mary Hannah."

She sat up and began to massage my thigh with her warm little hands, working her way down to my left foot.

"I saw your dad bring in your portable easel," she said smiling. "You painting again yet?"

"Not yet."

"You will. You'll be famous one day. The Gee will be famous. Your art will be coveted all over the world. I'll join you on the talk-show circuit and be one of those parasite groupies."

"I love it when you dream out loud."

෨ා

On a windswept March day, Mama Claire and I made the journey to her childhood farm at the edge of Savannah.

She and I were equal pilgrims of a sort, young and old versions of very similar creatures embarking on new worlds.

Two months shy of graduation with a bachelor's degree in fine arts, I was headed to Barcelona that June for a nine-month internship with a well-known painter. Excitement about my imminent work in Spain simmered just under the surface. I was living with gusto, which I found could be done completely sober. Physically, I was 95 percent myself. It was a mountaintop time with a bright horizon in all directions.

Mama Claire sat serenely in the passenger seat as the west Tennessee landscape slid by: rolling hills of small cattle farms and hobbyhorse fields, punctuated by trailer homes and the occasional gray-timbered barn, tin roof rusting with the passage of time.

"Grace, there's a liquor store up ahead. I need to stop and get a pint of scotch."

My jaw dropped to my lap, and I almost ran off the road.

"Honey, keep your eyes on the road. I was just kidding! We surely don't want any more accidents."

"Not funny."

"Had you going though."

"Still not funny."

"Sorry. Just wanted you to know it was OK to talk about it—joke about it even. Besides … we're in a dry county," Mama Claire said with an exaggerated wink.

"Well, maybe it's a little funny now," I said. It was surreal seeing my grandmother being such a cut-up. It occurred to me how rare a sight that had been for years.

"Mama Claire, how are you feeling, really? Do you sometimes feel the pull of it?"

"Honestly, I can't say that I'll never take another drink. But right now, I don't miss it. I feel like I have a really good chance to live a sober life, a more joyful life. What's left of it anyway."

"You do seem different. Better. Happier."

"Well, dear, I'm always happy to be with you. Maybe the trick is not to dwell too much on the past. I've learned—or hope I've learned—that the past can have the power to write the future, if we let it. It can create habits of feeling and doing to the point where you are lost. Before you know it, you're sixty-eight years old and wondering where it all went."

The truth of her words resonated with my own feelings of awakening from a distant dream, attention now fully focused, glad the nightmare was over and grateful for another round at life.

"I love you, Mama Claire."

"I know, sweetie. We are two peas from the same pod."

It was inspiring to see Mama Claire emerge from that lifelong chrysalis where she had hidden herself away for so long. Indeed, she *was* present. She was here. And she had brought a new person into our family, her roommate, Connie. We accepted her right into the fold. I think God brought Mama Claire and Connie together to discover something they could not have found alone.

It was a privilege to be with my grandmother on that journey, and I felt a sense of gravity as I came full circle with her. This was a final laying to rest. It was holy in a way—so much so that we didn't talk as we got closer to Savannah. We hadn't even told anyone where we were going.

I was about five the last time I'd been to the Steadman homestead, Mama Claire told me. Her mother had passed and we were all gathered up at the home before the burial. I couldn't picture the place, so as we pulled into a drive at the edge of a gravel road, I was nervous and expectant.

We reached the iron front gate, loose on its hinges, with twists and twines of sticky briars serving as nature's guards. A few lone daffodils bravely held court in the chill among the tangle. A wintery pasture stretched toward a distant tree line. The once-gracious family home, a Greek Revival structure with porches that wrapped around both floors and wide front doors, still looked inviting from where we stood.

"Oh, Mama Claire, it's beautiful. Why doesn't anyone live here now?"

"I still own it, dear, along with your great-uncle James. It sits on forty-two acres. We keep the taxes paid. A neighbor mows the pastures a couple of times a year and looks in on it from time to time. But it needs a lot of repairs to bring it back. Besides that, no one in our family wants to live out in the country in Savannah."

"I might. I really might when I get back from Spain. It looks like heaven to me. And I could bring it back a little at a time. I can already tell you I'm in love with it."

Mama Claire's laugh was as pristine as a bell's pealing. "I love your enthusiasm, honey. It tickles me to death. Seeing someone in the family bring it back would be a dream come true. I hope I live to see it."

"I really want to do it. I'm coming back here. The wheels are already turning. It almost makes me want to forget about Spain."

"No. You need to go to Spain. This is the time of your life to experience Spain. This old house has been here a long time, and it will still be here when you get back. If you're serious about fixing it up, I could deed my half to you in the meantime. And I'm quite sure we can work something out with brother James."

"Really? Oh, God, really?" I hugged her tight.

"Really."

"How are we ever going to get through all these briars?" I pondered aloud, laughing through tears.

"Now that is the question of the day."

We decided to leave my car and climb over a spot where the fence was down a few yards away.

"Don't know if my panty hose will survive this," Mama Claire quipped as she hiked up the bottoms of her double-knit pants and stretched her petite legs as far as they'd go. I loved her so much at that moment.

"You wear hose with pants?"

"Who doesn't?"

I had to laugh.

"Will the walk be too much for you? I'll find a way to open that gate."

"We're walking. You need to get a feel for your new property."

As we got closer to the house, I could see the disrepair, the rotten boards, peeling paint, mildew on the columns. But a good energy emanated—the aura of another time. Some of the brick steps leading up to the porch were crumbling at the edges, and brown leaves piled up high in the corners. It felt like home.

I could see my children someday laughing and running freely among the pin oaks. I'd sit on the front porch, watch them play hide-and-seek at dusk in the old pecan grove, and laugh at their high-pitched squeals when one of them was discovered crouching low in a shadow. I could see myself with an easel in the middle of a rolling pasture, capturing the light at the end of the day.

As Mama Claire rummaged through her purse to find the key, a vision of the old house in its heyday came to me as if I had been there—fires in all the fireplaces on a cold March evening, dinner at the long oak table, everyone buzzing with news of the day, music in the parlor after dinner, bedtime stories, and big, warm feather beds.

The front doors groaned as she opened them, one and then the other, revealing sky-high ceilings with ornate crown moldings and interesting, hand-hewed woodwork. A few rooms had stray pieces of furniture covered in old sheets, and the empty walls echoed past décor: tracings around the spots where paintings once hung, and period wallpaper, a faded floral print peeling along ceiling-to-floor seams.

Mama Claire was quiet at first, taking it all in. I'm sure she felt twinges of ghosts peeking in from other dimensions. After a time, she took my hand and showed me around, naming whose bedroom was whose, recalling her favorite books from the beloved library, explaining that the little room off the kitchen was where the help had their meals. Mama Claire said she liked to sneak into the "help room" and eat her dinner sitting on the cook's wide lap.

She told stories of parties and laughter and of times that were sad. Hers was a good life there, I could tell, full of cousins and houseguests, long horseback rides, quail hunts, close-knit family.

"Grace, I think it's time."

"Are you sure you're ready for this?"

"Ready as I'll ever be. I haven't been down there since the day I buried him, you know."

A chill ran down my spine.

As if on cue, the wind picked up as we started for the woods. Mama Claire's arm was hooked into the crook of mine, and we leaned into each other for warmth. Once amid the tall trees, the breeze lost its bite, and the density of the forest and undergrowth hovered around us protectively.

The sound of the creek reached us before we caught sight of it, and I heard her breath catch. We were near. I could see her on that long-ago day, cramping and bleeding, in shock, making the trek all alone, the towel-wrapped fetus pulled close to her breast. My heart bled for her.

When she saw the old cypress tree, she pulled away from me gently, a far-off look in her eyes. The ancient tree stood out from the others. It was grander, nobler. She ran her hands over the bark and down to the gnarly roots, feeling the tree's solid life force. As she knelt and placed her hands firmly on the earth, I knelt beside her and placed my hands on top of hers.

As we sat up, the sleeve of Mama Claire's blouse caught on something sticking out of one of the huge roots.

"Now what in the world is that?" she asked aloud, bending down for a closer look. "Oh my Lord, I don't *believe* it."

She began to sob as she ran her finger over the top of a metallic object protruding from a massive root.

"What is it? What's wrong?"

"My Lord. *Oh, my Lord.* Remember the cross necklace I told you about? The one I buried with him? It's here, Grace. Oh my. It's right here—grown right up into this old tree all these years."

There it was, indeed, a tiny golden cross, lodged upright into the smooth bark, as if it knew its job as a headstone, marking the grave of a brief and unconsummated life. We bowed in awe, unable to speak, knowing and feeling the purposefulness of the discovery. This was no accident, no freak of nature. Destiny was here, bringing the unbroken circle of Mama Claire's life into focus, providing us an altar to complete our pilgrim ritual, among the fraternity of spirits looking over and through us. I could feel them. It was love. It was love that had conceived that stillborn baby long ago, the remains now assimilated into Mother Earth. It was love that provided the lesson of being lost and found again. It was love that gave us this tribute, a symbol of the grander cycle of time where death is but a transition to a new perspective. This old tree was also a character in the tale, a living agent of God—no less so than the rest of us, all of us.

The Beginning

CPSIA information can be obtained at www.ICGtesting.com
Printed in the USA
LVOW06*2354061213

364264LV00002B/5/P